CARL TROUSER'S EDGE

BOOK ONE OF THE TROUSER TRILOGY

Cover Art by BeePea Design

carlleeuk.com

Dark Comedies by Carl Lee;

Trouser's Edge
Once Upon A Hell
Emery At The Gates

The Thing With Unreality

Knowing Things

Horror Fiction by Carl lee;

The Gangerwads

Etheren
From Vidium: The Second Book Of Etheren

I would like to thank every Emery Trouser on the planet for doing the type of job that I couldn't do myself because of all of the nonsense spilling out of my cranium.

CHAPTER I

It was a Monday morning like any other that Emery Trouser awoke to. The rising sun streamed through the floral net curtains in his bedroom warming up his face until it caused him to stir.

His eyes flickered open with protest only to be met by the light. He covered them with his hand, moaned and then looked at the clock on his bedside table.

6.44am.

As usual, he had awoken just a minute before his alarm was due to go off. He shook his head slightly and mumbled to himself whilst brushing his hand through his matted hair.

And then the alarm went off.

"For God's sake," he cringed. It was such an awful noise to meet with upon waking. As he leaned over to switch the alarm off, he fell limply out of the bed and banged his head on the radiator.

"Oh, bloody Hell!" he growled, rubbing his head.

Within minutes he was in the shower, trying in vain, *as always,* to adjust the settings to 'warm'. What was it with showers? He tried to think of any shower he had ever taken that had been fully to his satisfaction. There wasn't one. They were all either too hot or too cold. If he did manage to get one at just the right temperature the water came out in dribs and drabs or burst out of the shower head with such a velocity that it almost took his skin off.

Perhaps the perfect shower was a myth. They all claimed to be the best, power showers, super jet showers, deluxe showers, super-deluxe jet showers. They all simply lied. Either that or he was just unlucky.

And that was something he could well believe.

Emery wasn't a lucky man. He wasn't incredibly unlucky; he just wasn't lucky. His life was probably similar to many other lives that were being lived around him. He worked a forty-hour week, had four weeks paid holiday per year and got a relatively nice Christmas bonus in December. He played the lottery every week but had never won anything and yet every week he would still sit and wonder what he would spend his millions on.

But even his dreams were average. If he won the lottery, he might possibly buy a modest house in the country, a modest car and go on a modest holiday, somewhere not too hot. Infact, deep down he wasn't even sure that he'd like to win the lottery. It would really upset his routine. The jackpot would be a life-changing sum of money, far better for Emery that he would win a few hundred thousand pounds at most. That way he could keep his job as an accountant, stay in his humble apartment and continue living his inoffensive little life.

After his shower he sat at the breakfast bar in the kitchen, eating cornflakes and listening to the news on the television in the background. There was something about a mad cult leader in Russia leading his flock in mass suicide. He wasn't really paying full attention; he was too busy trying to eat the last of his cornflakes before they soaked up the milk and became soft.

Before leaving the apartment, he grabbed his briefcase and pulled on his overcoat, stopped to straighten his tie in the hallway mirror and then closed and locked the door behind him.

He commuted to work with an hour-long train journey into the heart of the city. He hated that part of the day. It was mainly because he wasn't fully awake and the cornflakes he had just eaten hadn't had chance to kick in.

And he hated trains full stop. They were always late, always dirty and always full and that was if they hadn't been cancelled.

Not full of nice, interesting people, that would be asking for too much. No, they were always full of drunken waifs snoring as violently as they smelled or idiotic teenagers trying to impress their equally idiotic friends by spitting bits of chewed up paper down the aisles.

6

He didn't let it get him down, infact he ignored it as best as he could. His grandfather had always taught him not to dwell on such things as they were trivial and wasting time on such petty distractions would ultimately leave him depressed and embittered. And it would most likely see him off to an early grave.

As he pondered the injustices of everyday life, what can only be described as a tramp sat in the seat next to him.

"Y'alreet pal?" spoke the man in a Scottish accent.

Emery simply nodded and returned his gaze to the window. *Why, of the handful of empty seats still available did he have to go and sit in that one?*

"Y' off ti' work?"

"Yeah," sighed Emery, over dramatically, as if to compensate for the tramp's lack of employment. "Bloody work!"

"Ah'd love ti have a job," replied the tramp, staring at Emery with steely eyes.

"Oh, yes, I mean, obviously…" Emery stumbled on his words. How could he have been so insensitive? There he was making a half-decent wage, complaining to a man with no money, no house and almost no hope by the look of it. "…I love my job very much. Have you… erm, have you ever had a job?"

"Aye, 'course I have. Used ti' clean the toilets oot on Sunnydale Street."

"That's great," said Emery, trying to inject as much enthusiasm into his voice so as not to offend the old chap.

"You think cleaning up other people's shite is great?"

"Well, no, not as such. What I mean is, it's great to be

7

in a job. Er, not that it's not great to not have a job but obviously it pays more to... you know..."

"How old ah ye? Aboot thirty?"

Emery nodded.

"Ah was aboot your age when my life went doon the swanny, and do ye know why?"

"No, why?"

"Because there was nay enough excitement in cleaning toilets, so ah went oot ti find some elsewhere. If only ah'd stayed on Sunnydale Street ah would nay be where ah am noo, sleeping in another man's strides and having ti piss all doon meself just ti keep warm."

"Things might look up, you never know," offered Emery, not really believing his own words but offering them up instead of an awkward silence.

"Aye, they just might," said the tramp as he stood, "this is my stop. Have ye got a poond?" he added.

"Yes, yes, there you go," said Emery, placing some change in the man's hand, "there might be enough for a breakfast or something."

"Arseholes ti' that, ah'm off ti' get pissed."

With that, the train screeched to a halt and the doors opened allowing the tramp to get off.

Emery shook his head and watched the man through the window as he staggered across the platform. He could almost see the smell trail lingering behind him.

*

Wormsley and Sons Accountants.

It was an average place of work, full of average individuals doing accounts. Emery had never really thought about his work. From leaving school, through college and ultimately to Wormsley and Sons, it was almost like his life was on autopilot.

Not that he disliked his work or his workplace. He simply had no real opinion of it at all. It was just something that he did. Numbers were the only thing he had ever really understood, they were logical. They never held any surprises because at the end of the day everything always added up. It all made perfect sense.

Numbers were safe.

He walked through the front door and through reception where he was completely ignored by the receptionist who, *as usual,* was doing her nails. He always wondered why she didn't do them at home. If she was so concerned with how shiny her nails looked surely she would have come to work with them already shiny. He gave it only a fleeting thought and then stepped into the awaiting lift. He pressed the button for the twelfth floor and watched the doors close.

As he stood, he counted the 'pings' in his head whilst daydreaming of nothing, to the warm thrum of the lift as it ascended.

The lift stopped on the ninth 'ping' and the doors opened.

There was no one there.

Emery peeked his head out of the lift and looked both ways down the ninth storey corridor but could see no one.

Puzzled, he stood back and again pressed the button

marked twelve, harder this time just in case he had only pressed it three quarters of the way in the first time. The doors closed and in a few moments he arrived at his floor.

As the doors opened, he saw the hurried bustle that was his office and began to make his way across the office floor to his desk at the far side of the room.

As usual, nobody gave him even the briefest of glances.

He arrived at his desk and turned his computer on whilst removing his coat.

"Hey, Trouser," shouted a colleague, "I hear Wormsley wants to see you in his office!"

"Big Wormsley or little Wormsley?" he asked, nervously.

"Big Wormsley," came the reply.

Emery stood in a moment of puzzlement and mild alarm. Why would Big Wormsley want to see him? Nobody got to see 'The Big Worm'. Sure, he had seen little Wormsley on the odd occasion, who hadn't? But never the Big Worm.

Emery calmed himself down a little, he thought back through the previous week's work and tried to recall if there had been any irregularities. None leapt to mind.

He started his slow walk out of the office and into the hall. For the first time, *possibly ever*, everyone seemed to be looking at him. He simply smiled a forced smile back at them. Did they all know something he didn't? Of course not. They were all merely as curious as he was to find out what the 'big man' wanted.

The fluorescent lighting flickered nauseously overhead as he wandered down the corridor, stopping in front of the door marked 'Wormsley Senior'. He knocked three times and waited. He felt dizzy with nervousness.

"Come in!" shouted the boss in a thick east London accent.

Emery opened the door to see an overweight, balding man in his early sixties sat behind a mahogany desk smoking a large cigar.

"Take a seat Mr…" he checked a piece of paper in front of him on the desk and read from it, "…Trouser."

"Thank you, sir," said Emery as he closed the door behind him and sat on the chair provided.

"You're probably wondering why I called you in here," said Wormsley as he puffed away on the Cuban.

Emery swallowed hard, "A little bit perhaps, Mr. Wormsley," he managed.

"Please, call me Horembrice," said Wormsley, coughing a large chunk of phlegm into his mouth and then spitting it out into the waste paper bin at the corner of his desk.

There was a moment of uncomfortable silence in which Horembrice seemed to make an involuntary whining noise that he somehow appeared oblivious to. Emery tried not to look directly at him and so turned his attention to the dead plant in the corner of the room. Where was that noise coming from? Was it his chest? Surely he could hear it!

The noise tapered off into a fine whistle and then ceased altogether. Emery presumed that now only dogs could hear it.

"How long you been working here, son?" asked the chief, his voice more of a smoker's growl.

"Erm, about twelve years, sir," replied Emery.

"Twelve long years, eh?"

"Oh, I wouldn't say they were long, sir," said Emery, trying to lift the stuffy mood in the room.

"No, but they were years and there were twelve of them," spoke the chief abruptly.

"Erm, yes, sir."

"Let's cut the small talk, shall we? I don't know you and, in all honesty, I couldn't give two tiny shit nuggets about you. I'm not a 'people person', Trouser and I never will be. I'm going to transfer you to floor thirteen. Special Accounts."

"Oh, right," sighed Trouser.

"You'll be working with Grindmott. He's expecting you, so get your shit together and get your arse up there pronto."

"Right, erm, thank you, sir," Emery wiped the worried beads of sweat from his forehead as he left the room. If he had known then what destiny had in store for him, he might have just left them there.

CHAPTER 2

It was around a quarter to ten by the time Emery had cleared out the contents of his drawers and put them into a box. Nobody had wished him luck or even so much as said goodbye. He didn't dwell on his apparent unpopularity though, he would be the first to admit that he wasn't a particularly sociable person, he couldn't see the point of it in the workplace. You were only there to work anyway. Besides that, the people in his office were a little too 'clicky' for his liking. They always had allegedly amazing gossip about other colleagues that always seemed highly dull and pathetic to his mind.

I mean, why on earth should he care if Margaret is dating Tony behind Colin's back? Surely the only person that that would be interesting to would be Colin, and he didn't even know anybody called Colin.

Or Margaret or Tony for that matter.

In fact, the more he thought about it, the more he was pleased to be leaving the pathetic banter behind him for the lofty heights of the thirteenth floor and it's 'special accounts'.

He picked up his box of belongings and made his way to the lift. There he paused for one last look at the twelfth floor and at all the people he had managed to avoid actually 'meeting'.

A brief moment later he sighed and pressed the button marked thirteen. Why on earth was he being so melodramatic? It wasn't as if he was never going to see the twelfth floor again. After all, that's where The Big Worm's office was.

The lift doors opened with a 'ping' to the thirteenth floor. Emery peered out on to a dimly-lit corridor approximately twenty metres long or so. At the end of it was a wooden door with a crudely fashioned sign announcing 'special accounts'.

As Emery left the confines of the elevator and began his walk down the corridor, he became aware of the fact that there were no doors at either side of him. *What then was the purpose of such a long corridor?* he puzzled. The insufficient lighting seemed to buzz eerily over his head and occasionally, it flickered as if his very footsteps caused to interrupt the flow of electricity to the bulbs.

As he neared the door, he noticed that the sign was a torn piece of card from a packing box and the writing had been scribbled on in crayon. It certainly didn't seem 'special'. He would have thought special accounts would be a little more prestigious than this. Maybe it was more elaborate on the inside, although even as he pondered this, he was somehow bracing himself for the worst.

He knocked three times on the door and opened it.

The room was probably quite large, although it appeared small because it was cluttered with wildly stacked files of varying sizes and it too was badly lit. The whole place was a labyrinth of books and ledgers and dusty shelves.

Emery closed the door behind him and began to wander through the maze, careful not to disturb the pillars of accounts flanking him from every angle. At the far corner of the room, in a catacomb of haphazardly stacked books shimmered a soft light and a man at the side of it scribbling away feverishly.

"Hello?" said Emery.

The scribbler stopped and looked up from his work.

"Ah, you must be Emery Trouser," said the man.

From the look of him, Emery assumed he was in his late fifties. His hair was a wild grey thatch and his face, a road map of stress, though his eyes portrayed a quiet wisdom somehow lost within the lines of age surrounding them.

"I am, yes."

"Good, I've been expecting you. I'm Grindmott. Or Hector, if you prefer." The man offered his hand. Emery leaned in to shake it but dropped his box of belongings on the floor.

"Oh, bloody Hell, sorry," said Emery, stooping to gather them up, "I'm not normally this clumsy. It's been one of those days today."

"Leave that for now, I've got something to show you," said Hector, standing.

Emery stood, looking slightly flustered.

"Walk with me," Hector motioned for Emery to follow him. "What do you know about special accounts, Emery?" he asked.

"Er… Nothing really. Nobody does," he said, walking to Hector's left.

"Well, I'd be surprised if anyone on twelve even knew there *was* a thirteenth floor."

Hector smiled.

"Yes, they are all a bit preoccupied with each other."

"Well, up here we handle the very important clients. Special clients. Secret clients."

Emery noticed the tone in Hector's voice. The way he had said *'secret clients'* had seemed to have an air of suspense draped over it.

"Secret clients?" he asked.

"Yes."

They stopped at an old, brown door that was tucked away behind a shelf of files.

Hector placed the key in the lock, but paused before turning it.

"The files in here are secret, Emery. They must not leave the room, nor must the information within them." His stare was firm and held until Emery nodded his understanding.

"Of course," the words stumbled out of his mouth.

"I know I'm throwing you in at the deep end, Emery, but you *were* hand picked for this job," Hector turned the key and the door clicked open, "So, I'm already assuming an element of trust here."

Emery swallowed to rid his mouth of the build up of nervous saliva, "I won't let you down, Hector."

"Good man," Hector opened the door and turned on the light inside.

The room was small and though almost empty, it still managed to look somehow cluttered. The wallpaper was peeling from the ceiling downward and the blinds were covered in so much dust, Emery imagined they wouldn't let any light in, even if they were open. In the middle of the room was a desk and chair and behind those stood a solitary filing cabinet.

"I was expecting something more," smiled Emery.

"Well, don't judge a book by its cover. Sometimes, the tiniest thing can have the loudest voice."

Emery walked over to the table and sat in the chair.

"Will this be my office then?" asked Emery. He had always daydreamed about having his own office. Not necessarily with a promotion, but merely his own space that wasn't overlooked by a dozen gossiping colleagues.

"Well, it's not technically your office. We'll both have access to the entire floor, but certainly you can work from here if you like. It is kind of cluttered outside."

They both smiled. Then, out of the corner of his eye, Emery noticed something etched into the tabletop.

The end is nigh

"What's this?"

"Oh, that's just a doodle," dismissed Hector. "Must have been the last fellow that worked here."

"Happy chap, was he?" said Emery, through a half smile.

"Not particularly. He had…" Hector paused, "…issues."

There was an awkward silence hanging between them, and then Emery moved the chair to stand. "Well, I'll bring my belongings in here then, shall I?"

"Why not? I'll go and put the kettle on and then we can get to know one another. No point in having two perfect strangers working in the same room, eh?"

With that, they both left the corner room for the maze of files in the main room, Emery stopping by the lamp to pick up his fallen materials and Hector continuing on to a makeshift kitchen area to rinse out two mugs.

*

"So, how long have you worked here?" asked Emery as he took a mouthful of tea.

The teabag had obviously been left in for far too long and the milk had been used so sparingly that it was barely worth gracing the mug with its presence. Emery had always been a fan of weak tea, it seemed far less offensive to the taste buds, even if it did, from time to time merely taste of hot water with milk.

"Well now," Hector scrunched his eyes and paused as if playing his life over in reverse, his mind the projector, the back of his eyelids the screen, "Thirty-two years, I think. Yes, thirty-two. I was twenty-five when I started."

"That's a long time, have you always been up here?"

"Good Lord, no. I had to work my way up here, much like yourself. I had to make a lot of sacrifices to get here too."

"Really?"

"Yes, we all have to make sacrifices in the end I suppose," Hector took a large mouthful of tea, as if to quell an emotion within.

"I suppose I'm the lucky one then," said Emery, "I haven't really had to make any sacrifices."

"Not yet maybe, but you will," Hector looked at him with a glassy stare that seemed to see straight through him but then snapped out of it and a warm smile flickered back across his face. "Or just maybe, you'll be one of the lucky ones, eh?"

Emery smiled. "I must say, you make your job sound almost scary. I've always found number crunching to be a safe job really."

"It is a safe job on the twelfth floor, but things are a little different here on thirteen."

"I mean, they are still just numbers though, aren't they?" Emery puzzled.

Hector sighed, "I suppose you're right, Emery," he stood, placing his mug on the desk. "Let's get you your first job shall we?"

19

CHAPTER 3

Emery walked into his hallway, closed the front door behind him and put his briefcase on the floor by the mirror. After hanging his coat up he sighed his way into the kitchen and switched the kettle on. It was at this point that he noticed a peculiar smell. He couldn't quite put his finger on where it was coming from but it smelled more than a little of rotting eggs.

His immediate response was to check the cooker for a gas leak only to realise an embarrassed moment later that his cooker was fully electric.

He opened the fridge door and sniffed all around the interior. There was nothing even remotely on the turn in there. And then, as quickly as the smell had hit his nostrils, it was gone.

The kettle clicked off, stirring him from his bafflement. He finished making his weak brew and took it, along with a box of cookies to the living room where he sank into the welcoming comfort of his settee with an exaggerated sigh of relief.

He grabbed the remote and a second later his television hummed into life.

The news was on.

More about the mad cult leader in Russia and the mass suicide of over a thousand of his followers. Emery shook his head with muted disbelief as the reporter in the field tried desperately to explain what little facts he actually knew. I mean, other than the fact that over a thousand people had killed themselves, what else was there really to report?

The media frenzy would now spend the best part of a fortnight analysing and over analysing the situation until they reached the inevitable conclusion that nobody really knew why they did it anyway. And at the end of it all, the people were still dead.

After flicking through a few more channels of rubbish he turned the television off and closed his eyes.

What a crazy place this world was.

Still, at least everything was going well in his world right now. A promotion. A new office, *well sort of.* He was going places, that was for sure.

His musings brought him warmth as he drifted quickly into an early evening nap.

His head lolled to one side, as did his cup of tea, which spilled gently onto the cushion beside him.

As Emery began to snore, the television hummed back

into life as a photo of the cult leader emerged on the screen. Blackened eyes seemed to pierce through the screen. Of course, Emery didn't see this because he was enjoying what would probably be the last good sleep he would get for some time.

*

He had awoken to find the stain on the cushion and had then tried to remove it with all manner of cleaning products, which he had newly discovered under his sink. However, none of them seemed to work, indeed one or two of them appeared to amplify the stain.

Eventually he had given up and made himself some tea. Why wasn't there some sort of universal cleaning product that could cope with anything? Who really had the space to store the seventy or eighty products required to deal with every cleaning eventuality? Not Emery, that was for sure. The cupboard under his sink was small and full of plastic bags. *Whose isn't?* He half smiled at the thought of that one fact alone uniting a nation, the common denominator that binds us all. The carrier bag collection under the sink.

It was an amusing thought but it wasn't getting his settee clean.

After his tea he had watched a smattering of television and had then gone to bed to settle down with a book. As was often the case, his eyes had tired and he had fallen asleep mid-chapter, the book becoming embroiled in the quilt. He would usually find the book the following night creased by his slumbering fidgets and have to reread most of what he had read previously.

3.45am.

Emery started awake with a loud snore and sat bolt upright in his bed.

It was still dark and he wasn't fully awake yet. Why had he woken up? He glanced at the clock and scratched his head for a moment and then he heard it.

A low, grinding crackle. What was it? Where was it coming from?

As he stood, the book he had been reading fell out of the bed with him, scaring him a little as it thumped to the floor.

"Shit!" he exclaimed. "Stupid bloody book!"

He walked slowly to his bedroom door and paused by the light switch, wondering whether or not to turn it on.

If it were burglars, the light would alert them to his presence. That could scare them away *or* on the other hand it could spark a confrontation and Emery was out of his depth in the realms of battle. Give him a sum and he could crack it. Give him an intruder and *he* would probably be the one getting cracked.

And there it was again. That noise.

It didn't sound like an intruder. There were no whispered voices or any sounds indicating that there might be people moving around. Just that low crunching sound.

He turned the doorknob and opened the door and peering his head around the corner he noticed the smell again. Rotting eggs.

He decided to put the hall light on, having almost

23

assured himself that he wasn't being robbed. Whatever was going on, it was going on in the kitchen. That was where the noise seemed to be coming from and that was where the smell had been earlier.

He slowly walked the short length of his hallway and peered into the kitchen.

As he turned the kitchen light on he was shocked to see a huge crack in his floor. It ran the full length of the kitchen and was around half an inch wide.

"Shit."

CHAPTER 4

"Subsidence!" said the landlord with a Cornish twang to his voice.

"Really?" asked Emery.

"Well, I can't think of anything else it might be. Fucking great crack in the floor, gotta be subsidence in my book."

Geoff Boils was a straight forward sort of man. In his mid-fifties, heavy-set with wild grey hair and bushy sideburns, he embodied the stereotypical Cornish farmer. However, he wasn't a farmer, he was actually quite a successful property developer and had been for several years now. As a landlord he expected his tenants to be straight with him and he in turn would be straight with them. A no-nonsense man.

"I suppose that's quite serious then, is it?" Emery knew the answer before he had even asked the question.

"I'd have thought so. I'll get on the old blower to a mate o' mine and see what's what. It don't look too good though, do it?"

Emery had called the landlord at half-past-seven, after hours of desperately trying to get back to sleep and failing. He had then called work and told them he would be late.

Wormsley Junior had answered and hadn't sounded too pleased, but then he never did.

It was generally the way with well-off people that they always seemed pissed off about one thing or another. He remembered something his granddad had told him years earlier. 'If you sit too long on a pile of cash, you'll end up just sitting on piles.' It hadn't made much sense at the time but had later caused a mild chuckle on reflection.

Moments later, the landlord had made his phone call and he shuffled back down the hallway and into the kitchen.

"Any luck?" asked Emery.

"He says he can have a look on Friday morning." Geoff pulled out a well used handkerchief and blew his nose. A comical trumpet noise emitted from within the rag.

Emery might have chuckled had he not been more than a little stressed and tired with his situation.

"Really, that late?"

"Well, he's in Mallorca 'til Thursday with his missus. Don't reckon she'd thank him for leavin' her there, do you?"

"No, I suppose not. I think I can work around it until then."

"Anything else while I'm here?" asked Geoff, now putting his 'full' handkerchief back into the pocket of his body warmer.

"Well, I can sometimes smell something a bit like rotten eggs. It's not all the time, just every so often."

"You been wiping your arse properly?" Geoff burst into a splutter of hearty laughter, "If something stinks o' shit, it's usually shit" he concluded.

Emery forced a smile, "It's probably nothing."

"Righto then, I'll see you Friday." With that the landlord waddled down the hallway and out of the front door, chuckling to himself as he went.

Emery sighed and looked at the kitchen floor.

Subsidence? That was all he needed.

*

Emery had arrived at work two hours late after a surprisingly pleasant commute. The train had been almost empty. The relative peace and quiet at that time of day, coupled with the side-to-side chugging had swayed him into a light doze from which he woke with a start. Fearing he had missed his stop he had almost departed the train two stops too early. Luckily, he had spotted the station sign on the platform and realised his would-be mistake in time.

Once at work he had taken the elevator to the thirteenth floor and joined his 'office mate' Hector who had put the kettle on to make his beleaguered colleague a good, strong cup of tea.

"So, Little Wormsley said you'd got a problem with your kitchen?" said Hector, pouring the water into the cup.

"Yes, the floor's cracked. Subsidence apparently."

Hector stirred the teabag around the cup and then scooped it out and discarded it into a rather full bin. It landed somewhere near it. "Subsidence?" He drew air in through his teeth. "Always bad news." He began to pour the milk into the cup.

"Can I have lots of milk please," said Emery, recalling the previous day's cups of tea.

A moment later Emery had his beverage and the two were chinwagging about the problems with modern housing.

Eventually, once the griping had subsided, Hector reached into a box and pulled out a file. He passed it to Emery across the table.

"What's this then?" asked Emery.

"Work, " smiled Hector, "We can't spend all day banging on about shoddy building techniques, can we?"

"No, I suppose not," sighed Emery.

Hector sat back in his seat and scratched his head.

"That is a special account Emery, so please be very careful with the numbers."

"I'll do my best, Hector," said Emery, not fully understanding why Hector was so concerned. It was very rare that Emery made mistakes and even on the odd occasion when he had erred, it was something very minor that had been easily rectified.

"Just pop it into the filing cabinet when you've done with it and I'll get you to sign off on it in the ledger afterwards."

Emery nodded his understanding and took the file to the small room at the back of the office. It was an uneasy room to work in, not least because it was cold and stuffy but also because of the lack of things in it.

One table, one chair and one filing cabinet, that now that he really studied it appeared to be bolted to the floor. That was very odd. Who on Earth would try and steal a filing cabinet? It would be nigh on impossible to steal anything from the twelfth floor without one of the Wormsleys sensing it leave the building, but up here on thirteen?

He placed the file on the desk and sat down.

The file was marked.

AL 3, 346 Borovski, goran

'*A L?*' Emery wondered. It was a passing wonderment only and he ploughed on through his work. It took around three hours to complete. There were very strange ways of doing a special account that Hector had taught him.

The run of the mill accounts were generally done to work out how much somebody owed in tax. As far as he could fathom, the 'special accounts' were worked out to see how much the person was owed. And on the few examples that Hector had shown him, there were no pound signs or mention of money at all.

Just numbers.

And the occasional use of those initials. *A L.*

He tidied the pages back into the file and walked around the table to the filing cabinet. He opened the top drawer to find it was empty. That was a surprise in itself as he had expected it to be at least half full. He put the file in and closed the drawer.

"All done," he announced as he closed the room's door behind him.

Hector looked up from his scribbling and smiled. "Jolly good, if you just sign off in the ledger that'll be you done for the day."

From under his desk he produced a thick volume of leather-bound, yellow-stained paper and placed it on the desk. After turning an array of pages, he settled on the right page and turned it to face Emery.

"Just sign my name, do I?"

"Yes, right next to the name of the account."

Emery signed his name and pushed the weighty tome back towards Hector.

"Can I ask you a question, Hector?" Emery was chewing his lip in contemplation.

"Of course," Hector placed the ledger back under the desk, "Just as long as it's not about building regulations."

Emery gave a half smile. "What do the initials A L stand for?"

Hector paused and looked slightly lost for words. "Erm… it's quite a long story really. Very boring and you don't need to know it to do the job. We should probably leave it there, I think."

Hector looked down to his work and continued writing.

"Okay. Well, there was one other thing."

Hector stopped writing again and looked up. "Yes?"

"The filing cabinet was empty. Is that er, right?"

The lamp flickered on the desk causing Hector to look slightly nervous. "The cabinet is emptied on a daily basis, Emery. Are there any more questions, only I am busy?"

"No, that's fine. I was just erm… you know, curious. That's all."

Hector nodded and smiled.

"I'll get off then, shall I?"

"Yes, I'll see you in the morning." Hector sounded friendly enough but he was now head in book. He had been very evasive and nervy of Emery's questions. Still, the whole thirteenth floor had always had an air of mystery about it, for those who knew that it existed. Maybe it really was none of Emery's business. After all, he was just paid to crunch numbers; did he really need to know *why* the numbers were being crunched?

He grabbed his coat and briefcase and began his long journey home.

CHAPTER 5

He had arrived home, eaten and settled down to watch the television as usual. He cracked open a bottle of beer and relaxed into the sofa, careful to avoid sitting on the tea stain, even though it was no longer wet. There was a nature programme on, something to do with crocodiles but he watched it without really paying attention, instead allowing his mind to wander.

What could A L stand for? Why did he even care? It was probably something obvious anyway. *Accounts Log?* But then, Hector had said it was a long story and 'accounts log' would surely have been a very short story.

His attention was grabbed momentarily by a crocodile chewing on some sort of antelope. It flipped the poor creature into the air and then grabbed it by the neck and wrestled it to the water. Impressive.

Alligator Lunch? Now that would be a long story.

As the antelope disappeared into the now blood-filled depths Emery heard a whirring noise from the kitchen. He muted the television to be sure. What the Hell was it?

He stood and peered around the corner of the wall that separated the living room from the kitchen. What he saw simply didn't make any sense at all.

The microwave was on.

'I haven't even used the microwave' Emery mumbled to himself.

He reached over to it and tentatively switched it off at the plug. As he did so the kitchen lights began to flicker rapidly. It was then when he noticed the smell of rotten eggs again.

He returned to the living room and picked up the phone.

There was a moment before he was connected to Geoff Boils.

*

It was quarter to ten before the landlord arrived.

Emery had let him in and had explained about the return of the smell, although that had dissipated shortly after. He had gone on to tell him about the microwave incident.

"Sounds like a power surge to me," Geoff explained, "They're quite common really."

Emery sighed. "Mr Boils, a microwave can't simply turn itself on."

"Oh, don't be so sure, lad, I seen it myself once. Not with a microwave mind. No, it was with a cement mixer."

Emery stood blank faced and silent for a moment.

"Well, what about the smell then? And no, I haven't forgot to wipe my arse." Emery was trying desperately to get to the bottom of the problem, but even he wasn't sure what he wanted to hear from the landlord.

"I'm not sure. Maybe there's a problem with the drains. I could give a mate o' mine a call." Geoff stopped there. He could see that Emery was stressed. "I don't know what you want me to say."

"I don't know either," Emery leaned on the breakfast bar and put his head in his hands, "I just want my kitchen to behave normally again." He gave a huge sigh and stood upright again.

Geoff stood in contemplation for a moment whilst casting a wandering eye over the crack in the floor. He ran a weather-beaten hand through his unkempt hair and scratched his head.

"I reckon I got it," he announced, "Quite simple really. The subsidence caused a crack, right?"

"Yeah," Emery sighed.

"Well, it's probably knocked a sewage pipe out of whack. At the same time, it might have knocked the electric off kilter."

Emery nodded, "I suppose that could be it," he conceded.

"Well, the good news is my mate can sort most of that out, even the electrics. He was a sparky for a short time, about ten years back. He had to do a few jobs to pay off some of his gambling debts." Geoff paused for a moment to let out a short burst of laughter, which in turn caused him to cough uncontrollably into his 'over used' handkerchief. "'Scuse me," he relaxed.

"And the bad news?"

"Well, like I said before, he aint back 'til Friday and it might be better if you didn't use the kitchen 'til then."

Emery appeared a little flustered. "How's that going to work?" he explained, "I at least need to use the fridge!" He thought for a moment as Geoff blew his nose. "Well, I suppose I can leave the fridge on and move the kettle and a few other things into the living room."

"That's the spirit." The landlord smiled. "Nothing's a problem 'less you think it's a problem, eh?"

"So, Friday's for definite, is it?" asked Emery.

"I reckon so. He's never let me down yet and I don't spose he's likely to start any time soon."

Emery tried to smile. He almost didn't dare to hope but what choice did he have? It wasn't as if the problem was going to solve itself and he didn't know the first thing about building work or electrics.

He said goodbye to the landlord once again and went back to the kitchen to begin moving necessities into the living room.

It was a little past midnight by the time he had finished. The kettle and microwave were now by the side of the settee, on top and beneath a nest of glass tables respectively. The tea bags and sugar now rested next to a handful of beers on the coffee table. He had

35

turned all of the other kitchen appliances off at the plug, all except the fridge and freezer which he was willing to leave to fate, rather that than let all the food spoil.

As he relaxed into the settee, he took a large swig of beer and turned the television on. He began to flick through the channels using the remote when the phone on the table beside him rang.

It was a bit odd that someone should call at this time of night. It was a bit odd that someone should call at all really. *Maybe it was important.*

He reached around the kettle and lifted the receiver.

"Hello?" he said.

"Is that Enkil?" came the reply, in a man's voice tinged with a cockney accent.

"Erm, no," said Emery, "I think you may have the wrong number."

"Doubt it, mate. Don't do wrong numbers." There was a silence as if the other were waiting for a response.

"Well, there's nobody of that name here and I've had this number for a good long while."

"Well, who are you then?" asked the man on the other end of the conversation.

"I hardly think it matters who I am," replied Emery, "the fact is, I'm not Enkil."

"I'm sure he gave me this number. Maybe he's late. I'll try back again later."

"Why? I already told you he doesn't live here!" exclaimed Emery, now becoming agitated with the telephone call.

But it was too late. The other person had hung up, leaving a dialling tone ringing in Emery's ear. He put the receiver back in its place and shook his head. What was it with wrong numbers? They always seemed to blame the person they had rung. *Could his day possibly get any weirder?*

He wouldn't have to wait much longer for his answer.

*

3.45am.

A clatter of pans?

Emery started awake in his bed. What now?

He looked at his clock. 03.45, the same time as the disturbance the night before. But this time it was different. That noise had been different.

He slowly and quietly edged himself out of the bed and crept to his bedroom door.

The minute or so that he was there, listening to a deafening silence, seemed like an age.

At first there was no discernable noise at all, but then there was a slight shuffling. It seemed to be coming from the kitchen. As he concentrated Emery was sure he heard whispering.

'Oh bollocks,' he whimpered to himself, 'bollocks, bollocks, bollocks!'

Now what?

What was the procedure for being burgled? There was no manual for this type of thing! You either had to grow some balls or get out of the house, sharpish.

Emery tried desperately to focus through the darkness to find a weapon of sorts to defend himself. *Was he actually going to do this? Was he actually going to confront criminals?* He wasn't thinking at all. It was as if he had switched on to autopilot.

At first, he picked up a belt from his trousers. It took him only a second to realise that he wasn't Bruce Lee. He discarded it just as quickly on to the bed.

'Bollocks,' he cursed again, under his breath.

He carefully opened the wardrobe door and quietly sifted through old trainers and clothes at the bottom of the wardrobe, desperate not to alert the intruders to his presence.

And then there it was.

At the back.

An old tennis racket.

Would that suffice? *It was heavy-ish.*

He smacked the edge of it down into his hand to try out its 'bashing potential'. It seemed hard enough. He wouldn't like to be on the end of it at any rate and that would have to do.

He slowly put on some trousers that had been haphazardly discarded at the side of his bed. He didn't want to face a situation like this in just his boxer shorts. That would be too weird, and this was weird enough.

He picked up the racket again and stood by the door. He waited and tried to listen again, hoping all the while that he was wrong. But he wasn't. He could still hear the whispers and shuffles from the kitchen.

Racket in right hand, he turned the knob of the door with his left, squeezing his eyes shut as he did so, the

38

main thought inscribed on his mind, *'bollocks'*.

And then he charged out of the bedroom and down the hallway to the kitchen, screaming like a wild man as he did so.

CHAPTER 6

"Aarrgghh!" wailed Emery down the hall.

His wailing soon gave way to silent horror however, as the kitchen quickly came into view.

Emery stopped in his tracks, his mouth agape and his eyes wide with startled disbelief.

The kitchen was bathed in a red smoking glow and through that smoke, the dark shadows of three men. Stood and silent.

Emery also stood silent. His mouth fell dry with shock and he found himself paralysed, rooted to the spot, his right arm still held aloft gripping tightly the tennis racket for protection.

The small part of his mind that was still working could offer no more than one word and it wasn't helpful in the least. *'Bollocks'*.

As the smoke cleared a little, Emery could see that the eerie red glow was emanating from the crack in the kitchen floor, which had widened considerably. The three shadows slowly became clearer and Emery gradually began to make out some of their features more clearly. It soon dawned on him that his predicament was only becoming worse with every passing second.

The man to the left was the shortest of the three, fairly stocky in build, short dark hair and a face smeared in mud. He appeared to be wearing some sort of army jacket that also seemed caked in mud. He smiled sheepishly as Emery looked him over.

The middle figure was the largest of the three. Well over six feet tall and well-built with it. His face was partly covered by long, black, matted hair but from what Emery could make out, he looked barely human. His face seemed like a sweating collection of scars and he didn't look particularly happy; stood proud, arms folded, no flicker of a smile across that ones face.

The third figure was wearing a dark suit, tall and skinny this one. Short, brown hair, cheekbones protruding from his sullen face, eyes sinking deep into his skull like two cavernous pits.

All three of them were looking at Emery, sizing him up as he sized them up and all the time Emery with his racket raised.

"Alright?" ventured the shorter of the intruders. His question sounded genuine enough.

Emery couldn't answer, his brain still hadn't rebooted. His mouth seemed to half form a word but nothing audible came from within. *Just as well*, he thought, *he could probably only say 'bollocks' anyway* and that might offend them.

41

"Erm, did we wake you?" this from the shorter one again, fidgeting now, seemingly uncomfortable and embarrassed at being caught out.

The fog of shock had gradually begun to ebb from Emery's mind and the occasional flicker of intelligence crept in to take its place. Though he could barely hope to believe what he was seeing.

"Er," Emery coughed a little to clear his dry throat, "Yeah, you did wake me."

The shorter one looked at his colleagues for a brief moment and then back to Emery.

"We're sorry about that," he scratched his head. "We erm, we didn't know you'd be in."

Emery lowered the tennis racket slightly and blew out a great sigh of air as the final waves of shock left him. He was silent for a moment as he seemed to survey the situation in front of him and then, "What the Hell is going on?!"

And then he passed out.

*

As he came to, Emery could smell rotting eggs. It was almost enough to put him off waking up. He opened his eyes and found himself staring up at his living room ceiling.

The television was on in the background. He listened

for a moment. It was some kind of 'red hot late' channel.

He tried to think back. *What had happened?*

And then he remembered and shot bolt upright on the settee.

"Alright, mate?" said the man in the army jacket.

"What's going on?" panicked Emery. He frantically looked around for the other two but they weren't there. Not in the living room anyway. He turned his gaze back to the one who *was* there, sat in the chair, holding the remote.

"You were out for a good half hour, thought I'd watch a bit of TV," came the reply.

Now that Emery looked, he could see the man more clearly than before. He didn't look at all well. His skin was an off grey, caked in dirt, as were his clothes and his eyes appeared drawn and black.

"I don't mean what's going on with the TV, I mean what's going on? Why are you in my house?"

"Right, yeah." The man rubbed a filthy hand across his face, smearing the dirt there. "Well, that's a long story, mate." His accent seemed to be northern, possibly the Lancashire area, though Emery was no expert on dialects.

"Try me," he insisted.

"Right, well. Where to start?" he coughed into his hand. "My name's Enkil by the way."

Emery recalled the name from the phone call earlier. "I'm Emery."

"Well, Emery, some of this might sound a bit out of the ordinary but I'll do my best to simplify it for you," Enkil continued, "just try to keep a bit of an open mind, yeah?"

43

Emery nodded. *Was this actually happening?* He pinched his arm, just in case.

"Erm, I'm afraid we've had to commandeer your kitchen ,mate." The statement was quite frank. Void of humour, it was a statement of fact.

"What for? Drugs?" Emery hadn't grasped the situation at all.

"Drugs? Not unless you've got some, even then, I'm not sure they'd do much for me."

"Why? Are you ill?" Emery was growing more nervous by the minute.

"Bit more than ill, mate. I'm dead."

There was quiet. It seemed like for a long time too.

Emery grabbed a bottle of beer from the coffee table and twisted the top off. He paused for a moment and then took a massive swig from it, finishing off more than half of the bottle at once.

He looked at Enkil. "Beer?"

Enkil half smiled, "Why not?" he knew this would be hard work.

Emery passed him a beer and Enkil opened it. He sniffed at it first, "I probably won't be able to taste it but I'll give it a go anyway." He took a healthy gulp and his eyes lit up. "Oh, that's good. That's really good." He immediately took another swig. "Can't taste a thing down there." He added.

Emery tried to process the new information. "So, you're dead?"

"Yeah."

"Well, that would explain the smell," stated Emery.

"Whiff a bit does it?" asked Enkil.

"Just a little bit."

44

"Yeah, sorry about that. We don't get many showers down there. Water shortages and all that."

"Down there?" asked Emery. He took another swig of beer. "So, you're a ghost then?"

"No, I'm just dead," replied Enkil, also taking another swig of beer.

"But, you're from down there? Hell?"

"Yeah."

"What's it like down there?" Emery noticed some of his nerves subsiding. Only some of them but he felt a little more at ease, no less confused though. The beer was helping to take the edge off things, he only hoped he had enough in stock. He was expecting a long night.

"It's not bad, I suppose. Well, it used to be okay. It's gone to shit a bit at the moment, that's sort of why I'm here."

"Oh shit, it's not my time, is it? I'm not ready yet..." Emery started to panic.

"Relax, man, it's not your time. Well, as far as I know anyway."

Emery sighed a gust of relief into his beer bottle as he tipped the last of it down his neck. "Why *are* you here then?"

Enkil paused before replying.

"Like I said, it's a long story." He leaned forward. "There's a bit of a war going on down there at the moment, you probably don't need to know the ins and outs of it, but we have it on good authority that your house is of some strategic importance. We don't know why yet. We're trying to figure it out as we go along."

"So, you ripped a hole in my kitchen?" asked Emery.

"Yeah, sorry about that. It's a result of the portal

making process. There's a lot of energy required to make a portal. It sometimes causes side effects."

"And even you don't know why you're here?"

"We only know that we *have* to be here. We get most of our information from an oracle of sorts. Very clever woman. She used to be a witch when she was alive, then she got burned at the stake. That's when her career really took off."

"A witch?"

"Yeah, there's quite a few of them down there. Most of them are full of shit, but the one that works for us is never wrong."

"She works for you? So, who do you work for, what do you do?" Emery was trying ever so hard to take all this onboard but it still seemed so fantastical that he knew it would take a while to fully sink in.

"Well, we work for the Committee of the Northern Republic of Hell. The CNRH for short. Intelligence work mainly, a bit like the FBI or MI5." Enkil took a swig from his bottle and then leaned forward in his chair. "All this is a secret by the way, top secret. So please don't tell anyone."

"Who would I tell?" Emery half laughed, "If I did tell anyone I'd probably get locked up in the nut-house!"

"There is that."

"So, Hell's a republic? What about Satan?"

Enkil laughed. "Satan was a long time ago. Hell's been a republic run by an elected committee for centuries now."

"Isn't Hell supposed to be horrible and... flamey?" Emery wondered.

"Well, it is quite flamey in parts, but it's not really that horrible. Not once you get used to it. I mean, it's tough when you first get there, but if you knuckle down and do what you're told you can move through the ranks and end up in a good place."

"Are you in a good place?" Emery finished his beer and reached for another one.

"I *was*. The CNRH is a good job, but not at the minute. Dangerous times right now."

"Really?" Emery began to feel uneasy again.
Dangerous Times? Did that mean he was in danger?
"Am I in danger?"

"No. The portal's a secret. We have guards on the Hell side of it and there will always be someone here on this side too. You should be perfectly safe."

"For how long? I mean, I have a life, you can't stay here!"

"I'm afraid we have to. It's out of my hands, but just as soon as we know why this address is important, we'll be out of your hair as soon as we can."

"I can't believe this is happening," said Emery pushing a worried hand through his hair.

Enkil finished his beer and put the empty bottle on the coffee table. "Listen, try and get some rest. You might feel better after a good sleep."

"I can't sleep with all this going on! Hell's cracked open my kitchen and I'm talking to a dead man. I doubt I'll be sleeping for a good long while!"

"You should try all the same."

Emery knew he was right.

CHAPTER 7

Emery awoke slowly and sluggishly. The quilt was too comfortable for him to want to leave it. He wallowed in the softness of his pillow, gathering the edges of it and pulling them around his head. As the mists of sleep slowly dissipated, he found himself staring at his clock.

09.55am.

"Oh shit!" he started.

How had he overslept? Why hadn't the alarm gone off? Maybe it had and he hadn't heard it. That was possible, he had been really tired after the night he'd had.

And then it all came flooding back to him.

The portal. The strangers. Dead people. From Hell. In his flat. *Did all that really happen?*

He rushed on some jogging pants from out of his

wardrobe and hurried himself through his bedroom door and into the hallway. He could see from there that the crack in the kitchen floor was indeed wider, but gone was the smoke and the red light. He walked through the kitchen, scouring the sides with his eyes, and into the living room.

And there was Enkil.

He was eating a bacon sandwich and watching cartoons on the television.

It *was* real. All of it.

Enkil spotted him and heard his defeatist sigh.

"Alright, mate?" Enkil asked. "I made myself a bacon sandwich. I had to use the microwave. It still tastes good though. Better than the rubbish down there, you want one?"

"No," Emery replied, "No thanks, I'm not hungry."

"Should never skip breakfast, it's the most important meal of the day, you know?"

"I'm just not in the mood," Emery sighed again, "And I'm late for work." And then he wondered. How could he go to work? He had all this happening to him in his flat, how could he even contemplate work? That was the last thing he needed. Presuming he did go to work, how on earth could he possibly concentrate on numbers and figures knowing that there were a handful of dead people waiting back at his flat guarding a portal to Hell?

Enkil continued eating his bacon sandwich with royal delight. Obviously food with 'taste' was in short supply in Hell. "This is good bacon, mate." He smiled and took another bite whilst returning his attention to the cartoons.

"I'm going to ring in sick, I suppose," said Emery,

sitting down on the settee and reaching for the phone.

"Might be better to go in really," said Enkil.

"Why?" worried Emery.

"You know, life as usual. That way, nobody's going to suspect anything."

"I very much doubt me calling in sick would give rise to the suspicion that I had a portal to Hell in my flat. At worst, they might just assume that I'm not ill and merely want the day off. Besides, I'm already late."

"It will do you good to get out of the house. You know, get some perspective on it all."

Emery thought about it for a moment. What good would staying at home do? If these people were going to be here for quite a while; he couldn't take too long off work, could he? He would have to go about his life as usual. Ignore the Hell thing and get on with it. He almost laughed. *'Ignore the Hell thing?'* That might be easier said than done. Still, there was no point in him staying in, there was little or nothing he could do about the situation, so he may as well go to work.

"You're right," he concluded. "You're not going to do anything while I'm out are you?"

"Like what?" asked Enkil.

"I don't know... sacrifices or Satanist things?"

Enkil took another bite of his butty and chuckled to himself. "It's really not that sort of deal, mate."

Emery returned to his bedroom to get dressed, still uneasy about leaving the house.

*

He arrived at work at lunch time.

The receptionist was still filing her nails, albeit whilst eating a sandwich and talking to a friend on the phone. That must be the 'multi-tasking' that women seemed to talk about so often. No wonder that they got so good at it. It was all the practice they got at work.

He took the lift straight to the thirteenth floor. Hopefully Hector wouldn't be too upset with him and hopefully he hadn't felt the need to tell Little Wormsley. Being late once a week would have been bad enough but twice would probably deserve some sort of 'dressing down' in the office and Emery was in no mood for a ticking off. Not today.

As he walked the long corridor to the office he noticed that the humming overhead fluorescent lights seemed to be even louder than he remembered them. Maybe it was the lack of quality sleep, he did feel more than a little strung out. The lights weren't helping. "Bit late, aren't we?" asked Hector as Emery entered the room.

"I'm really sorry," he offered, "I got here as fast as I could." Emery put his coat on the back of a chair and headed for the tea making area. "You fancy a cuppa?"

"Why not," shrugged Hector, looking up from his sandwich as Emery switched the kettle on and rinsed two mugs in the small sink. "Kitchen trouble again?"

Emery gave out a small nervous laugh, "Yeah, you could say that."

It didn't take long for Emery to finish making the tea, sitting opposite Hector once he had done so.

"Thanks," said Hector taking his cup of tea from Emery and taking a sip. "Bit milky," he noted.

"Yeah, sorry. I must have slipped with the milk,"

51

Emery replied, smiling inwardly.

"Well, there are two files for you to get through today. There were three but I did one earlier." Hector slid two files onto the table towards Emery. "They shouldn't take too long really, they're quite slim ones."

"No problem," said Emery, tasting his tea. It *was* quite milky.

"So, when's your kitchen getting fixed then?"

Emery had to think for a moment. "Well, er… it was supposed to be Friday, but now I'm not so sure."

"New developments?"

"In a manner of speaking," he nodded. "The subsidence has got worse anyway."

And then a worrying thought occurred to him. What if the portal was still there on Friday? The landlord and the 'builder' were due round to sort out the *subsidence.*

Only, it wasn't subsidence and no amount of cement could fix the problem, surely.

You can't simply concrete over a doorway to Hell. And even if you could, how could he explain the dead people walking around in his flat? The simple answer was that he couldn't.

"Are you alright?" asked Hector, noticing how pale Emery had suddenly become.

"Er, yes. Yes, I'm fine." Emery snapped out of his pondering. "I'm still a bit tired, that's all. I didn't get much sleep."

"You should try hot chocolate. That always sends me off a treat."

"Yeah, I just might." Emery sighed. If only it were that simple.

CHAPTER 8

Emery had finished his work by 4.30pm and had then made his way to the train station for his journey home. He had made it just in time to avoid the huge downpour that was still in effect.

He sat under cover, on a wooden bench and stared out into the rain as it beat down and bounced off the track. His mind was swimming with stress. His main problem was that he still didn't believe what was happening to him. *How could he?* A portal to Hell in his kitchen! Who *would* believe it? Until yesterday, he hadn't even believed in ghosts or anything even remotely paranormal. Of course, it *had* happened and indeed was still happening.

He was half entertaining the notion that he was possibly going mad when a person sat on the bench beside him. The smell was a familiar one.

"Y' alreet pal?" came the gruff, Scottish tones.

Emery turned to see the tramp that had sat next to him on the train two days earlier.

His weathered and unshaven face seemed dirtier than before and his smell seemed somehow damper. But then, he had probably been caught in the rain.

"Ah, hello again," Emery smiled politely.

"Pissin' it doon, eh?"

"It is, yes," he agreed, silently willing the train to hurry up. He wasn't in the 'talkative' mood today. Too much on his mind.

"Rain's flaring up my feet something chronic. Blisters are shoutin' at me arse, tellin' me ti sit doon!"

"It's typical British weather!" Emery forced a small laugh.

As he looked down, Emery noticed that the tramp had taken off his shoe and was picking at the blisters on his reddened, wet foot. He winced at the smell of warm vinegar wafting over towards him.

"It's probably time ah got some new boots, eh?" said the tramp, still heavily engrossed in his sorry excuse for 'preening'. Emery's eyes were drawn to the shoe that the tramp had removed, as it lay there on the bench. Its tattered toe end obviously hadn't stood a hope in Hell's chance of keeping water out. And there was that word again. Hell. He couldn't get away from it, even with a tramp's bare and blistered foot in his face.

Ironically, maybe *that* was Hell. It certainly wasn't pleasant by any stretch of the imagination.

"How's that job o' yours goin?" asked the tramp, now reaching for his shoe and putting it back on again.

"Er, fine." Emery didn't really know what to say. "How… are you going?" he eventually added.

"Well, last neet ah had ti sleep in a skip, 'cos some bastard had boarded up the shit hole ah normally crash in. Then ah had ti puke in a bowl just so ah had somethin' ti eat. Just my luck that there was nay even any chunky bits."

Emery was lost for words. I mean, how could he possibly respond to that?

"Other than that, I'm peachy."

"That sounds… harsh," managed Emery, and then "I've probably got a few pounds spare if that will help?"

"Aye, it might," replied the tramp as the oncoming train began to roll up to the platform. "Ye' could pay me on the train if the conductor comes round."

"Er… ok," said Emery. He cursed inwardly, knowing full well that the tramp would undoubtedly sit next to him.

Both stood from the bench and waited for the train to come to a stop, which it did to the sound of protesting brakes.

"After you," gestured Emery, as the doors hummed open.

"No, you first, pal," the tramp said politely.

Emery stepped onto the train and walked into the carriage to his left, the tramp followed.

The carriage was empty, apart from an old lady at the back who looked as if she had just woken up. Emery sat at a section with a table, onto which he placed his brief case. The tramp sat opposite, fidgeting as he settled.

"Underpants climbin' up ma shitter," he cursed as he pulled at his trousers with his grubby fingers. Emery cringed internally at the mental picture that had quickly formed and deformed in his head.

They sat in silence for a few moments as the train shuddered to a slow start and continued its journey. Emery gazed through the window to the driving rain outside. It rolled across the window in chaotic beads and along with the rhythmic chugging of the train, he felt almost hypnotised.

"Ahm Jack by the way," spoke the tramp, stirring Emery from his thoughts.

"I'm Emery," he replied.

"Emery?" Jack snorted, "Christ! What kind of name is Emery?"

Emery shuffled uncomfortably, "It's a bit of a strange one, isn't it?" he managed to smile.

"It's a fuckin' beauty!" he laughed. "I've heard a few strange names in ma time but that just aboot takes the biscuit! Mind you, ah once had a pal called Genghis."

"Genghis?" Emery smiled.

"Aye, that's a pearler, isn't it? God knows why a parent would do that to a child they've not had time to hate yet."

They both laughed.

"So, what do you do Emery?" enquired Jack.

"I'm an accountant."

"Aye, ah figured you for a job like that. Ah was never any good wi' numbers. Well, ah shifted a couple o' number two's when ah worked on Sunnydale Street but you catch ma drift." Emery nodded. "Ah always fancied being a singer. You know, in a rock band, but it's a tough old business the old 'rock game'. *And* ah could nay really sing. It was more of a growl really. People

56

just thought ah was shouting at them."

"I was always just good at numbers," said Emery, "I never really thought about it much. I just woke up one day and I was an accountant."

"You never fancied being a rock star or sumthin'?"

"No, I don't think so anyway. Maybe a scientist when I was really young."

"Aye well, you probably did the right thing, eh?" Jack looked out of the window at the rain drenched countryside rushing by. "Beats beggin' oot in all that."

Emery found himself feeling slightly sorry for the tramp and even a little guilty for not wanting to be bothered by him. Ordinarily, his worries paled in to insignificance compared to Jack's. A few pounds here and there to buy off the guilt and to steer away another man's problems all of a sudden didn't seem to sit right with him. However, these days were far from ordinary for Emery and quite possibly his own problems were no longer insignificant, and that thought alone allowed him to shelve his guilt.

At that point, a conductor opened the door to the carriage and wandered through. He stopped at the old lady first and asked her for her ticket. Emery couldn't be sure but he sounded Russian. That was a new one, a Russian conductor. He supposed it wasn't particularly odd in itself, living relatively close to the city, there were all sorts of ethnic groups and people from all over the place. But there was something strange about the conductor. Something a little unnerving. He couldn't quite put his finger on it. Maybe it was the way the man had looked over at Emery before turning his attention to the old woman.

As the conductor turned from the old lady, Emery noticed how unwell the conductor looked. Sunken eyes, pallid skin and a feverish forehead. All of a sudden, he felt extremely uncomfortable.

"Are you alright, pal?" asked Jack, noticing how pale and uncomfortable Emery looked.

Emery didn't answer. He knew that something was wrong here. He just didn't know what.

The conductor stopped at the side of the table where Emery and Jack were seated and stared at Emery. "Tickets," he spoke sharply, his gaze never wavering.

And there *had* been a Russian tone to the voice. How was that important? He didn't know that it was, but it did somehow add to his discomfort.

"Two to Heaton Croft, please," asked Emery, taking some money out of his pocket.

"Heaton Croft?" questioned the conductor.

"Er… yes." Emery was nervous now and his voice trembled slightly.

"Are you deaf, pal? The man wants ti go ti Heaton Croft," Jack had piped up, seeing how nervous Emery had become at the presence of the conductor. And then Jack noticed it too. The man wasn't looking at all well. And his clothes didn't seem to fit properly either. He was easily several sizes too big for them.

The conductor now turned his steely gaze towards Jack.

"Are you Emery Trouser?" came the growling Russian voice.

"Ah might be, who wants ti know?" Jack stood slowly and stared coolly into the Russian's eyes.

"Emery Trouser is an enemy," growled the conductor.

And then he grabbed Jack by the throat, his fat fingers squeezing around the skin of his neck.

"Fuck you!" shouted Jack, head butting the Russian. He loosened his grip on Jack's throat straight away and reeled backwards into the opposing table crunching into it and falling into an unconscious heap.

Emery was rooted to his seat with shock.

Jack looked over at Emery who looked completely bewildered by what had just happened. "It's alright, Emery. He's on his arse."

"What the Hell was all that about?" he blurted.

The words had barely left his mouth when the Russian began to stir from within the heap of fat and broken table.

"Might be best to get off the train," said Jack. "Pull the emergency stop lever!"

Jack pointed to it, just behind Emery's head. Shock gave way to urgency and Emery sprang into action, leaping over the back of his seat and banging his chin on the table there.

"Oouucchh!" he shouted.

"Might want ti hurry it up there!" Jack yelled as the Russian's eyes opened.

Emery reached up and yanked hard on the lever and immediately the brakes screamed into action causing everyone in the carriage to lunge forward. The old lady, who hadn't been paying attention to the melee, shot forward in her chair and smacked her head on the table in front of her.

Jack and Emery went flying down the aisle and both came to a painful halt at the door to the carriage.

Finally the train squealed to a halt and Emery and Jack

scrambled to their feet.

"Grab your case and let's go!" ushered Jack.

Emery did so and they both quickly opened the two doors that lay between them and their getaway.

Jumping down off the train and onto the tracks proved a little too much for Emery who fell and dropped his briefcase. He thought about trying to retrieve the case, which had found its way under the train, but then thought better of it and ran after Jack, who was already climbing the grass banking towards the open fields that lay ahead.

They both clambered up the embankment and over the small wooden fence that lined the field on the other side.

For the next five minutes, they ran, rarely looking back to see if the Russian was giving chase. He wasn't, but they wanted to put as much distance between him and them to be on the safe side.

They slowed to a tired walk and tried to catch their breaths.

"What the Hell was all that about?" gasped Emery, his cheeks reddened from his sprint.

"Ah thought you might already know. The guy there seemed ti know you."

Jack stopped to look back over the fields they had just raced through.

"Well, I've never seen *him* before!"

"Tell me, how does an accountant become '*an enemy*'?" Jack smiled as he stressed the last two words.

CHAPTER 9

After trudging over numerous sludgy fields in the rain, they had eventually found a telephone box next to a village road where Emery had proceeded to call a cab. Ten minutes later they were out of the rain and on their way to Emery's flat.

Waiting in the rain had given Emery time to play back the recent events in his head.

He still wasn't sure why a fat Russian dressed as a train conductor had it in for him but he was sure that if Jack hadn't been there, he may well have been in a lot of trouble right now.

"Thanks for what you did back there, Jack."

"Nay bother. Ah've tackled worse than that fat gonad. It's no picnic fightin' over a left-over pizza with a bunch o' pissed up tramps by the way."

Emery smiled, "Well, thanks anyway. I'm not much good in a fight."

"Have you ever been in a fight?" asked Jack.

"Er… no, I don't think so."

"Then how do you know?"

Emery thought for a moment and then shrugged. "I suppose I don't really."

"You never know 'til you've tried. Ah think you'd probably handle yourself okay if push came ti shove."

Emery gleaned some sort of pride from Jack's comment. It wasn't every day that he received a compliment. Or even an acknowledgement of any kind. Infact, it was sort of nice just to have a conversation with someone.

"Well, if you want, you're more than welcome to come back to mine. I can sort you out with some food; you can get a bath if you want. I might even have some clothes to fit you." The offer was a genuine one, not out of pity but out of gratitude and Jack sensed this.

"Aye, why not? Ah could do wi a clean set o' strides and a hot meal. You're a good sort, Emery."

It was only then, at that point, that Emery remembered the 'state' of his flat. The truth was, he hadn't actually forgotten, merely pushed it to the back of his mind in order to absorb what had just happened on the train. Now that it had dawned on him, how could he possibly take Jack back to his flat?

"Actually, my flat's a bit of a mess," he panicked. The words just spilled out of his mouth with little or no thought required.

"Ahm nay fussy 'bout a bit o' mess. It'll make a nice change from sittin' in dog shit, just ti keep mi arse from getting cold on the floor."

"Yes, I suppose…" *Of course!* Why would a bit of mess put a homeless person off coming round for tea? Emery was running out of ideas. He, himself *had* to go home. He was soaked and muddy and needed to change and he also needed to ask Enkil a few things. On the other hand, he couldn't very well drop Jack off on the way after being the one who had just invited him. Especially after what the man had just done for him. There was only one thing for it. He would have to tell him something, make up a story. *But what?* My flatmates are always dressed for Halloween? No, Jack was homeless, he wasn't stupid. *What then?* Maybe he could tell Jack the truth. After all, he was a man of the world; he'd probably seen his fair share of strangeness.

But there was strange and then there was 'strange'. All the time he was thinking, the taxi was making its way ever closer to his flat. He would have to throw himself in the deep end and hope for the best.

"The thing is…" Emery began, "I'm having a spot of bother with my flat at the moment. Try to bear with me on this because, it may sound a little hard to believe."

He paused, barely believing what he was about to say. "There's a portal to Hell in my kitchen." And there it was, out in the open. But then something Emery didn't expect.

"I know," replied Jack.

*

63

Emery unlocked the front door to his flat and both he and Jack walked into the hallway. Emery could see the kitchen and see that the crack in the floor was still there. *Did he really expect otherwise?*

"Come through," he motioned to Jack. "Make yourself at home." They turned left into the living room where Emery came face to chest with a huge, very dead looking man. Actually, he couldn't be sure if it was a man at all. The face, partially covered by dark, matted hair was scarred intensely with eyes that burned a deep red. He remembered this one from the night before. Of course, he had then fainted in a very non-heroic manner, something that he felt could readily happen again.

"Ah…" he started, "er… hello?"

"Ah, Emery, don't mind Bodin there, he's a bit keen that's all." Enkil said from somewhere behind the hulking pillar of demon.

Bodin stood, arms folded, staring down at Emery in a way that made Emery feel very small and insignificant. That wasn't too hard to achieve, Emery had spent most of his life feeling slightly insignificant. Not normally in his own flat though.

"Does he move?" he enquired.

"Bodin," called Enkil, "it's Emery, let him in."

The beast grunted and moved to one side allowing Emery and Jack to pass.

"And you must be Jack," said Enkil, after biting into a bacon sandwich.

"Aye, that's me." Jack leaned forward and shook Enkil's hand.

"They told me about you at HQ. Good to have you onboard, mate, although if you're here, I'm guessing

64

we've got problems?"

"Yi' could say that."

Jack sat down on the settee whilst Emery disappeared into the kitchen, returning moments later with a six-pack of beer from the fridge.

"Beer anyone?" he offered as he sat. Both Enkil and Jack nodded and reached for a bottle.

Jack had disclosed a few nuggets of information in the taxi on the way home, though Emery wasn't really sure if he had understood any of them. He had revealed that he had a 'talent' for talking to the dead.

"Had it since ah was aboot nine," he had said. "At first ah thought ah was imagining it but after a while it became much clearer, y' know… the voices an' that. A wee while later, ah realised ah could talk back and they could hear me. Ah've been talking ti 'em ever since. 'Course, ah never told anyone. I did nay want folks ti think ah was mad. As ah got older, ah started ti help a few 'spirits' oot here an' there. These days ah'm pretty busy 'cos there's a lot o' shite going on *doon there*."

Emery had understood that part at least, mainly because the 'shite' had spilled over into his kitchen and had very much upset his day-to-day routine.

Jack had gone on to explain that he had been asked two days previously to co-operate in a matter of the utmost urgency. Quite literally a matter of life and death.

He hadn't had time to elaborate, as the taxi had then turned the corner to Emery's street.

"So, you work for Enkil?" puzzled Emery, taking a swig of his beer.

"Not exactly," Jack began. "Ah kind of work for the

65

Committee of the Northern Republic of Hell, just like your pal here, but ahm nay dead. Ma talent means ah can keep an ear oot for enemy communications. That's how ah bumped in ti you at the train station." Jack paused to take a drink of his beer and then continued. "Ah'd intercepted an enemy message so ah knew something was going doon. All ah had ti do then was locate where the message was going ti and follow it. And hey presto, you, me and a fat, dead Russian on a train."

Emery nodded his understanding.

"So, you actually engaged with the enemy?" asked Enkil, his mouth full of bacon and bread.

"Aye, he tried ti kill me. Ah dropped the nut on the bastard though. Knocked the smile oot the back of his face." Jack chuckled to himself.

"It's started then. We're going to have to be extra vigilant from now on!" said Enkil.

"There's two more things that might be important," Jack went on. "Firstly, the Russian knew Emery's name. That's *why* he attacked. He called him the enemy."

"He knew your name?" This was directed at Emery now.

"Er… yes," worried Emery.

"And did you recognise him?" asked Enkil.

"No."

"Then, the oracle was only half right. It would seem Emery, that it's you that's important, not this flat."

"The other thing," Jack interrupted. "The fat guy knows where he lives. Ah mean, not the address but he knows we were going ti Heaton Croft."

"That's bad," Enkil bit his lip in contemplation for a

moment. "But Heaton Croft's a fairly big place. It will take them a while to sniff out the portal and that at least means we have *some* time to play with." He ate the last mouthful of his sandwich and rinsed it down with his beer. After letting out a huge belch he continued. "I'll let the committee know what's happened and then me and you are going to have to talk," he concluded, looking at Emery.

Emery sighed inwardly, wondering just how much worse his situation could possibly get.

CHAPTER 10

It was a little after eight o'clock when Jack emerged
from the bathroom. Emery had taken his bath first,
delighting in scrubbing the sludge from the fields off
him and then soaking for ten minutes in the hot,
steaming water. The bubble bath had helped too.

He rarely used it. Infact, he rarely used the bath at all.
A shower was far more convenient amid his general
routine but a bath had been the ideal relaxant under the
circumstances and the bubbles had been the perfect
allies to it.

Similarly, Jack had almost fainted as he lowered
himself into the steaming water. He couldn't remember
the last time he had taken a bath but assured himself it
couldn't have been more welcome or any way near as
heavenly as this one. Outwardly, you wouldn't have put

Jack down as a fan of bubble bath but he almost cried as he lay there, the bubbles gently popping around him, the warm water lapping at his chin. It became a chore to move at all as his muscles relaxed so entirely, let alone actually go through the whole rigmarole of getting washed.

As Jack walked into the living room, Emery was stunned by the transformation in him. The clothes he had laid out for him seemed to fit quite well, a purple shirt, black trousers and belt, and a pair of black shoes that Emery had long since stopped wearing.

Emery also noticed that Jack seemed much younger than he had previously thought, mid to late forties infact. *It must have been all the dirt*, he mused. Now, with clean-brushed hair and clean skin and clean clothes he actually seemed quite regular.

"How do the clothes fit?" he asked him.

"Great. Shoes are a bit tight but hey, ahm nay complaining." His smile said it all. "You sure ah can keep these?" he asked, looking down at his new clothes.

"Yes, no problem. I don't wear those any more anyway."

"You're a top lad in ma book, Emery. And that bath! God, that felt so good ah could have shit biscuits!"

Emery smiled at the notion of someone actually 'passing biscuits' and said, "Well, there's a chicken curry here," pointing to the plate on the coffee table. "It's a microwave one I'm afraid, the cooker's offline at the moment."

"Ahm nay bothered aboot that, ah could eat a battered nad, ahm that hungry."

Jack sat beside Emery on the settee and started to dig into his food with all the grace of a malnourished dog. Emery continued eating his own curry, trying to ignore the slurping noises to his left.

A brief moment later, there was a flash of red from the kitchen accompanied by a great whooshing noise and Enkil was back from the 'other place'.

"Scrubbed up well, Jack," he noticed upon entering the living room.

The two looked up to see Enkil in full camouflage gear now, not just the jacket. He also had a series of rather sinister looking daggers and machetes attached to his belt.

There was something in his body language too, something of more urgency about him. The situation was obviously direr than Emery had thought and this staved his appetite almost immediately.

"So, how bad is it?" he asked, placing his fork onto his plate. Jack had no such trouble and continued ploughing the food into his mouth.

"It's not good, mate," Enkil sat on the chair to the left of the settee. "We may be running out of time and it seems the enemy are one step ahead of us. We didn't expect them to be anywhere near finding out about the portal let alone discovering where it is. Now, we still have the upper hand there, for the time being at least, but they also know about you, something that *we didn't* know until a few hours ago. That means their intelligence is good, so we need to get our intelligence up to scratch too. And that starts with you, my friend."

Emery looked lost. "But I don't know anything. If

you're relying on me for your intelligence, you're in more trouble than you think."

"You may 'think' that you don't know anything but if the enemy are after you, you must be a threat to them somehow and we need to know why."

Emery sat quietly for a minute, thinking as hard as he could about anything and everything on the off chance that something would present itself to him.

Next to him, Jack finished his food with a deep, rumbling burp and dropped his fork onto the plate.

"That was spot on!" he exclaimed, slumping back into the chair and undoing his belt. "Any chance of another beer, pal?" he added.

"Yeah, just dive in," Emery said. "Do you want one?" he asked Enkil.

"No, I better not," he replied. "Are you going to finish that curry though?"

"No, carry on." He pushed the plate over to Enkil and wondered if he had ever seen Enkil without food. He didn't think so. Maybe there wasn't any food in Hell. *Having said that if you're dead, do you really need to eat?* He would have to ask him at some point, and many other questions besides. And then he had a thought.

"Well, hang on a minute. I'm trying to think about what I may or may not know and I don't even know about what *it is* that I may or may not know about!" *It made sense in his head.* Enkil looked slightly bemused. Jack merely took a swig of beer and stuffed his hand into his trousers. "Maybe if you told me exactly what was going on, I might be able to figure out what it is I might know."

Enkil placed the plate of curry on to the coffee table.

71

He realised that Emery was right, but didn't really know where to start. It was a long story.

"Alright, I'll start at the beginning." He paused for a second to gather his thoughts.

"Hell's a very complicated place. Since the Committee came to rule a few centuries ago, things sort of changed from the old routine of torture and infinite torment. It had to change really, mainly because Satan had let things get a bit out of hand. You know, there were too many souls going in to Hell and what with the endless torture thing going on, it was impossible for the souls to redeem themselves and the consequence of that was that Hell was getting a bit crowded."

Emery reached for a beer and cracked the top off it.

"Yeah, go on then, I will have one," said Enkil. "Thirsty work, all this talking."

Emery passed it over and then opened one for himself.

"So, when the committee came about, they created something called 'the points system'. I mean, there's no call for money in Hell, but some sort of pecking order needed to be put in place. People needed to know where they stood. The more points they earned the better a person's standing was. Eventually, a soul can earn enough points to redeem himself and maybe get sent to the 'other place'. Either that or they can at least be reincarnated on Earth as a badger or something."

Emery nodded as he took a swig from his beer. Jack did the same.

"I mean, it depends why you're down there in the first place. The committee don't shirk on the torture thing completely, you know. But someone like me, well, if I spend the next five hundred years or so working for them I can earn enough points to give the other place a shot." Enkil now took a swig from his bottle, swallowing over half of its contents in one go.

"Why, what did you do?" asked Emery.

"I robbed a lot of people. Did a few bank jobs too. I could tell you that I was a victim of my own environment and waffle on about never having a proper upbringing but truth be told, I was a bit of a dickhead in life. I always wanted things I didn't deserve, never wanted to work for a living and I wasn't smart enough to invent anything and live off the royalties. It was just easier to steal stuff. I'm learning the hard way now though."

"Am I going to Hell?" asked Emery, a slightly perturbed look sitting on his face.

"I've no idea. I doubt it though, you don't look like the sort, but then again they never do." Enkil smiled and finished his beer.

"God, I can't believe I'm having this conversation. What's happened to my life? I'm actually asking a dead person if I'm going to Hell!" The incredibility seemed to hit Emery in waves and this was a big one.

"Think yourself lucky, pal," spoke Jack. "Ah had the same conversation with maself when ah was ten!"

"This can't happen to many people, can it? I mean, why me?" Emery put his head in his hands.

"That's what we're trying to find out."

He sighed and looked up at Enkil again, "Yes, of course. Sorry, I still haven't really got my head around the whole thing yet. I don't really want to, to tell you the truth."

"Well, if it helps get you through, think of it like this. You don't really have a choice."

"Thanks," said Emery sarcastically. "That helps a lot."

"Right, where were we?" Enkil thought for a moment. "Oh yeah, the points thing. Well, and here's where the trouble starts. The CNRH have been investigating certain souls for a kind of 'points fraud' for some time now. Certain souls seem to be acquiring points, seemingly without having earned them. This means that a selection of lowlifes are accruing more power than they deserve and obviously the committee don't like that."

"Canny bastards those criminals, eh?" said Jack.

Enkil continued. "Well, we caught a handful over the past few years. They're in a lot of pain right now. The torture chambers that run under the Abomination Plains are no place for the faint-hearted. Satan had them built about half way through his reign but the committee liked them enough to keep them on. Still, nobody's spilled the beans yet, so we're still in the dark as to how they are getting the points."

A thought occurred to Emery that he was currently sat in the most surreal history lesson ever. *He hoped there wasn't going to be a test on it later.*

"Anyway," Enkil went on. "When they heard we were clamping down on them, a bunch of these souls pooled their resources and they're a pretty powerful bunch as a single unit. Points mean power. They've got a lot of sympathisers too, which didn't help our cause at all. They amassed a small army that we've been fighting for the last six or seven months and we *were* getting the better of them. And then, a few days ago something happened that we didn't expect. Slarin. A Russian maniac. He was some sort of religious cult leader who convinced his sect to commit suicide with him so that they could seize power in the afterlife."

"I heard about that, it was on the news!" exclaimed Emery, just happy to understand something for a change.

"Yeah, well, he not only had over a thousand newly dead souls already enthralled to him but he and his followers have a massive amount of points and took over the enemy's army. The other thing is, they just let him. It was like they had been waiting for him to do it. The committee hadn't planned for a coup and now we're really up against it!"

Emery pondered for a while.

"But I don't know about the Russian, apart from what it said on the news and I wasn't really paying attention to that to be honest. I've never met the man in person."

"There has to be something! Slarin wants you dead, Emery and that means you know something that he doesn't want us to know." Enkil stood now and paced around in a circle. "There has to be something. Has anything happened recently that you thought was maybe out of the ordinary?"

"You mean, apart from a portal to Hell opening in my kitchen?"

"Yes, apart from that."

"And apart from being attacked on a train by a dead Russian?"

Enkil stopped pacing and gave Emery a serious look. "Can we take this seriously, please? It's not just my arse on the line here. The enemy want you dead, you know?"

"You don't have to tell me that!" insisted Emery, "I mean, Christ! I'm an accountant for God's sake! This kind of shit doesn't happen to me every day. My life was great!"

Enkil frowned a little at him.

"Alright, maybe it wasn't great, but it was good enough for me. I was going places too; I got a promotion on Monday. Not much more pay, but I moved into a better office. Well, maybe not better but…"

And that's when something clicked. He wasn't sure what at first but he realised he had hit upon something.

"You alright?" asked Enkil.

"Hang on," said Emery as he sat in deep contemplation. It looked to the others like mild shock or sudden bafflement.

"Have yi just shit yourself or somethin'?" Jack asked.

"My promotion."

The other two waited.

"What about it?" Enkil eventually asked.

"Well, now that I think about it, it is a bit weird. I mean, it's different to what I normally do. The numbers, the letters, the whole style of accounting is very different to what I'm used to."

"Sounds a bit thin to me, mate. Is there anything else?"

"No, it's not just that. The office, there's something a bit odd about it. The files are moved every night and when I asked my colleague about it, he seemed… evasive, like I shouldn't stick my nose in. I shrugged it off at the time but it did seem strange, you know, the way he acted."

"It's as good a place as any to start," said Enkil,

retaking his seat.

"What do you mean?" puzzled Emery.

"Well, you need to ask your colleague again, only this time you need to get some answers."

"How do you propose I do that?"

"Well, I'd tie him to a chair and set fire to his feet. Failing that you could always cut a couple of his fingers off."

Emery looked horrified. "Are you insane? Who do you think I am, Al Capone?"

"I'm just suggesting… look, you do what you think's best, mate but one way or another we both need those answers!"

Emery knew he was right but he wasn't about to start torturing people to get to the truth. A truth that just might have little or no bearing at all on his present predicament.

"Is it even safe for me to go to work?" asked Emery. The thought occurred to him that there might be several people watching the train stations for him.

"Take a cab there and back and take Jack with you too."

"Eh?" Jack protested. "Ahm a fuckin' eavesdropper, pal, not a bodyguard!"

"Sorry, mate, but I can't very well go, can I? I think I might stick out like a dead person in a crowd full of living people! Besides, you're perfect, you can 'listen' out for the enemy."

Jack sighed. "Fuck it. It's nay like ah've got anything else planned!"

CHAPTER II

Wormsley and Sons Accountants.

A place that until now, Emery had considered safe and mundane. Usual and routine.

A place that had now taken on a different form. As he looked at the building through the rain-spattered window of the taxi, he noticed that the building itself appeared oppressive and foreboding; its tall, gothic exterior seemed less a romantic feat of architecture and more a looming hulk. Maybe it was the rain driving as it did, so relentlessly through the overcast sky that made it feel so oppressive, or maybe it was that Emery was beginning to realise that he was perhaps a pawn in a very dark game. And whatever game was being played, there was a strong possibility that at least part of it was being played right there.

The previous night, Enkil, Jack and Emery, after deciding to 'improve their intelligence', had continued to talk for a few hours over a handful of beers, discussing the plans for the morning after. Emery hadn't been particularly happy about having to go to work, regardless of whether he avoided the train stations or not. Jack too, had been similarly unhappy with the assignment of becoming a bodyguard to Emery, but had resigned himself to the fact upon realising that he was the only man that could realistically do the job.

All of this seemed redundant to Emery now as he sat, staring out of the parked cab.

"I'm not so sure this was actually such a good idea," he said nervously as he fidgeted in his seat.

"Aye, but what other choice do we have?" Jack was sat next to him, dressed in his old clothes again, muddy and worn. "Look at it this way, the sooner you're in, the sooner you're oot." He gave a half smile that Emery found only half reassuring.

He paid the taxi driver, took a deep breath and they both exited the cab and stepped out into the rain, hurrying quickly into the covered doorway of the building.

"So, you'll be right here then?" asked Emery, reassuring himself of the plan.

"Aye, don't be too long, eh? It's fucking freezing." Jack rubbed his hands together and blew in them to keep them warm.

"I'll do my best. You keep an ear out for… dead Russians," he never thought he would hear himself say that.

Without further ado Emery walked into the building

leaving Jack outside to keep watch. He looked out onto the bustle of the street as people made their way to work in the blustery shower. It was going to be tricky 'hearing' anyone coming through the crowds of people that were scurrying up and down the street.

Emery strolled by the receptionist, who wasn't polishing her nails for a change, and made for the elevator. He nervously scanned the lobby for anything or anyone out of the ordinary. It all seemed like work as usual, on the ground floor at least.

The lift doors opened and he stepped inside. After pressing the button marked 'thirteen' he watched the lift doors close and took a few deep breaths as it carried him skywards.

What was he going to say to Hector? Emery wasn't at all keen on pressure situations, he normally avoided them completely, but the last week was proving to be one pressure situation after another. Maybe it was karma. He had avoided these moments practically all his life and now he was getting his share of them in one solid chunk!

He tried to calm his thoughts by taking a few more deep swallows of air.

On the ninth 'ping', the doors opened.

Why did it keep doing that? "Stupid bloody thing!" he mumbled under his breath. He peered out onto the empty corridor and cautiously looked to his left and then his right.

Nothing. There were a few doors further along the corridor, but nothing remotely suspicious. He re-pressed the button for the thirteenth floor and a moment later he was there, out onto the long corridor leading to special accounts.

As he opened the door to the room, he could see Hector scribbling away in his usual place at the far corner of the room.

He closed the door behind him and weaved his way through the pillars of books.

"Becoming a habit, this lateness," said Hector without looking up from his work.

"Yes, sorry, Hector. Unfortunately, I can't stay long either."

Hector put down his pen and looked at Emery. He noticed that he looked more than a little tired and that his hair hadn't been brushed either.

"Late night?" he enquired.

"It's the kitchen thing again, I've got the builders in this afternoon," Emery lied.

"Oh? You should have rung in and taken the day off, you needn't have come all this way."

Emery sat down opposite Hector. "Oh, it's no problem"

"Cup of tea?" asked Hector, looking down at his own cup and finding it almost empty.

"No, thanks." Emery paused and wondered how to begin the 'interrogation'. "Hector, I need to ask you a few questions if you don't mind."

"Sounds serious," said Hector, noting the tone of Emery's voice.

"Well, it might be. How much do you know about what we actually do here?"

"Accounts?"

"No, I mean, up here on thirteen. The accounts are

81

different here."

Hector paused and studied Emery's eyes. "Are you in some sort of trouble?"

"No, I just…" Emery struggled for words, "I just don't know what it is we're doing up here and I find it all a bit strange. I mean, I always used to know what I was doing downstairs and I never had any problems down there."

"And you're having problems up here?"

"I just want to know what we're doing, that's all."

Hector fiddled with his mug on the table, swishing the remnants of his last brew around the bottom. "Emery, if you're in some sort of trouble, you should tell me."

"I'm not, I'm just curious."

Hector sighed and let his mug rest, "I've been here for a good many years now. I wasn't always in special accounts, in fact there wasn't even a 'special accounts' back in those days. Not that I know of anyway. I got this job because I don't ask questions, Emery and neither *did* you. I have my own theories of course, but I don't ask because I don't need to know and furthermore, I don't want to know. Now, I don't know why you're suddenly so curious about the whole thing but I strongly advise you to let it go. Some things are best left alone."

"Surely there must be something you can tell me?"

"I can tell you that the last person who started asking questions disappeared. One day he was here and the next he was gone." Hector looked hard at Emery, "What we do here is important, Emery. I know that much. Important and secret. That's all we *need* to know and if that's not enough for you then maybe we picked the wrong man?"

Emery thought deeply. Hector knew more than he was telling, of that he was certain but there was no way he was going to give anything up. Whatever it was, it was serious enough to lay down a threat of sorts, however subtly it had been made.

"You haven't got the wrong man," Emery forced a smile, "I've just been under a lot of stress with this whole kitchen thing. What with that and the new promotion, I just want to be able to do the job properly, that's all."

"Well, you needn't worry there," Hectors face lightened up slightly. "You're doing a fine job. Now, go home and sort your kitchen out. Take tomorrow and the weekend off and start back Monday, refreshed."

"Okay, thanks, Hector." That at least would take the pressure off him for a few days. He might be able to concentrate more on the 'job at hand' if he didn't have to think about work for a while. On the other hand, he hadn't learned anything at all about the accounts and he felt more positive than ever that they were somehow involved with what was going on.

As he left the office, he pondered that it had probably been a wasted journey and that if it had been Enkil in his shoes, he may well have left with the information he had wanted. And possibly a couple of fingers. He sighed; torture was just something that didn't sit well with Emery. Surely there had to be another way?

As Emery walked through the lobby and out through the doors, he noticed that Jack had resorted to begging in front of the building in order to keep warm.

"Jack?"

Jack stopped harassing a suited gentleman and turned

83

to face Emery. "Ah, thank God for that, ahm freezing ma tits off!"

"I thought you were supposed to be keeping a low profile?"

"Ah was. Who's going ti suspect a tramp of anything? Besides, ah've earned a tenner while you've been in there!" Jack pulled out the coins from his frayed pocket and showed Emery.

Emery nodded, "Very impressive," he managed, dryly.

"Alright smart arse, how did you get on then?"

Emery stood in the rain now at the kerb, his arm held out to hail a cab. "Well, I think he knows something, but he's not letting on."

"Not letting on? Is that it?" Jack sounded stunned. "We came all the way for that? Did you nay set fire ti his feet?"

Emery gave him a knowing glance.

"For Christ's sake man, do you want me ti ask him? Ah'll kick the answers oot of him, nay problem!"

"I don't think that will be necessary but thanks for the concern," Emery put his arm down as a taxi pulled up to the kerb. "Come on, let's head back."

"Okay, but I don't think Enkil's going ti be satisfied."

They both entered the cab through the same door and after a moment they were on their way home.

The journey took a little over half an hour but Jack had fallen asleep after just five minutes, which left Emery to his own musings. The last week had been a lot to take in.

A week that had started so promisingly with a promotion and had somehow ended up with not only a portal to Hell in his flat, dead people staying there, a befriended tramp with a natural flare for talking to the dead, but also a breakaway army of the dead after him. It was difficult to imagine just how much worse a week could get. Not that he was trying to imagine it getting worse, his primary thoughts were focused on improving his situation. He wasn't having much luck in that area either, the best he could come up with was to run away. In itself, it wasn't an idea completely without merit but he reasoned that Hell would find him wherever he ran. Better then to focus his attentions on finding out just how he was involved in all this.

It was clearly to do with Wormsley and Sons, that much was obvious now, but how did he himself fit into the picture? It had to be special accounts. Hector's reaction to questioning had surely confirmed that, but what was so special about them?

There had to be a way of finding out.

His thoughts were broken as the taxi turned onto his street. He stared through the window at a car parked across the road from his building. He could make out two dark figures in the front seats, though the rain made it difficult to make out any discernable features. Any other time and he probably wouldn't have noticed at all but these were strange times and he couldn't take any chances.

"Er, don't stop, just drive on, please," he quickly said to the driver.

"Where to?" the driver asked.

"I don't know yet, just carry on down the street."

Jack stirred, perhaps unconsciously sensing the heightened alarm in the car. "What's goin' on?" he said as he sat up straight.

"I'm not sure, I think there's someone watching the house." Emery's eyes never left the suspect vehicle as they steadily approached it.

"Where?" Jack's eyes now nervously scanned the road ahead. "Right across from my place." He nodded toward it as he spoke.

Jack's mouth seemed to dry in an instant. He closed his eyes and concentrated hard on the road ahead, focusing on any 'other worldly' mind-jargon that might be emanating from the parked vehicle.

"Anything?" worried Emery.

"There's nay noise but… it's weird, a kind of static fuzz." He opened his eyes again.

"What does that mean?"

"Ahm nay sure, but ah've nay heard it before. It could be nothing but it does nay feel right ti me."

"No, me neither."

The pair sat back in their seats as the taxi drove slowly past the car, Jack's window closest to them. They continued down the road and then turned left, on towards the cemetery, just under half a mile along the same road.

"Did you get a look at them?" asked Emery.

"Aye, ah took a fuckin' photo as well," he replied sarcastically. "'Course ah never. That would have given us away, do you not think? Me gawping through the window! You may as well just get oot and ask if they're here ti kill you!"

"Shit!" Emery struggled to focus. "They've found me, I'm a dead man!"

"Just calm doon, eh? You're not dead yet. Think aboot it, if they're watchin' the place, they're not sure whether it's right or not. If they were sure they'd be in there already."

Emery seemed to relax a little. "Yeah, maybe."

"Listen, we'll stop up here and call Enkil from the next payphone, eh?"

"Okay," he agreed. "There's one on the corner of the cemetery up here."

They continued on, the black cab cutting a sombre shape through the curtain of rain that fell on them.

CHAPTER 12

The chapel stood proud from the surrounding graves, though the rain clouds overhead dampened its serenity somewhat. The clock on its north face indicated that it was just past noon and Jack wondered how much longer it could possibly keep raining at this pace.

He was standing outside the phone box at the corner of the cemetery, rubbing his hands and tapping his feet on the pavement to keep warm whilst Emery made the call home.

Emery had plied the phone with change and dialled the number. It was on its fourth ring and still no one had answered.

"Come on, come on," he mumbled, his agitation spilling over his calm.

Finally, it stopped ringing and Enkil answered.

"Hello?"

"Enkil? It's me, listen. There's someone watching the flat."

There was a moment's pause at the other end as Enkil considered the information.

"Where are you?" he eventually replied.

"Not far, but we can't come back. Not now."

"Where are they, the watchers?"

"There's a black car, out front, across the road. We didn't get a good look, but I think there are two people in it. Jack did a scan thingy and he said it was weird, not normal. What shall we do?"

"Stay put for now," Enkil sighed. "Call me again in an hour, I'll try and work something out."

"Okay," replied Emery, a little disappointed that Enkil didn't have an answer ready for him there and then.

"Oh, by the way, any joy at work?" Enkil quickly added.

"Not really. There's definitely something not right there though and I think it's to do with special accounts. Hector was even more cagey than before."

"Didn't go with the torching of the feet then?"

"No."

"Okay, don't forget, call back in an hour. I'll sort out a plan of action."

Jack watched as Emery hung up the phone and stepped out of the phone booth into the rain.

"Well, he said to stay here and ring him back in an hour." He scrunched his coat collar around his neck to stop the rain trickling down his back.

"That's great!" he scanned the graveyard until his eyes

settled on the chapel. "Let's go in there, ahm soaked!" They scurried through the open gate and down the winding path that split the graveyard into two, finally reaching the covered entrance to the chapel.

"Jesus wept!" Jack shouted, clearly annoyed at his relentless soaking. "Is it too much ti ask for a bit of sunshine?" He tried the chapel door but to his even greater annoyance it was locked. He simply turned to Emery and looked at him with quiet disbelief.

Emery sensed that his Scottish friend was close to breaking point and Emery wasn't far behind him.

"Listen, it's okay. We're sheltered enough here for now. It's just for an hour."

They stood in silence for a few minutes, looking outward over the gravestones haphazardly scattered at either side of the path. The rain showed no sign of easing; indeed, it was bouncing off anything it landed on with seemingly increasing force.

Just then, a huge explosion of thunder boomed above them, causing them both to jump. "Fuck!" they both shouted almost in perfect synch and then looked at each other with wide eyes.

"That sounded pretty close," said Emery looking back out to the graves.

Before Jack could answer a bright flash of lightning struck the tree opposite with an enormous crack.

"FUCK!" they both shouted again.

A second later a smouldering crow fell stiffly from out of the tree and lay next to a gravestone, smoking.

They looked at each other again, though this time there were no words. Not for a good ten seconds, until the shock had subsided.

"What were the odds of that happening?" asked Jack, his eyes now fixed firmly back on the scorched carcass.

"That..." said Emery. "...was an unlucky crow."

They remained there, staring at the crow for what seemed like an eternity. "Wait…" said Jack.

Emery looked as Jack closed his eyes and concentrated.

"What is it?" he worried.

"A voice. Ah think someone's trying ti speak ti me."

It was barely audible through the rain but the more he concentrated the clearer it became.

…Wormsley and sons. Can you hear me? It's Wormsley and sons!

"Ah can hear you… crow?" asked Jack, still clenching his eyes tightly shut.

Crow? Who's Crow? I'm Richardson, Alan Richardson; I used to work there, until I found out what was going on.

"Go on," prompted the Scot, trying to shake off the image of the crow.

Emery's in grave danger and if you're with him so are you! It's special accounts, they go straight to Hell!

"What do you mean?"

The accounts are for dead people. They pay a fortune before their deaths and somehow the money is then converted into points to take over to the other side! The voice was rapidly becoming rushed and more distant.

"Wait, what's happening?" Jack struggled to concentrate harder.

It's not you Jack, it's me. I'm sorry, my energy's running out.

"Can ah help?" Jack asked, desperately trying to keep

91

the spirit talking for as long as possible.

Not unless you can bring me back to life. Listen, tell Emery, it's the filing cabinet. It has some sort of link to Hell. Destroy it and you destroy the enemy's access to power!

Emery looked on with bemused interest.

"Thank you," Jack's shoulders seemed to relax slightly as the voice began to fade. "But why? Why are you helping us?"

Because the enemy destroyed me.

There was a cold silence for a brief moment.

Oh and be careful when you destroy it, watch… out… for…

"Watch out for what?" Jack repeated himself but he knew it was too late. The spirit had faded. "Bastard! Can ah not catch just one fuckin' break?"

The massive crack of thunder overhead answered his question.

*

Enkil peered cautiously through the floral net curtains in Emery's bedroom to the street outside. Sure enough, there it was. A black car perched on the opposite side of the road. He couldn't quite make out how many figures were in the car partly because of the rain and partly because of the net curtain he was looking through. He daren't move it though in fear of being spotted.

He walked back to the living room where Bodin was stood waiting.

"Well, there's a car there alright. At least two people in there that I can make out." He sat on the settee and thought for a moment. This was serious.

Bodin grunted his unease.

Enkil scribbled something on the back of a paper bag that had once been home to a bacon and cheese pasty and handed it to Bodin.

"Okay, here's what we do. You go through the portal and give this message to Anders. He'll consult the council and come back through the portal with you, with the plan of action. In the meantime, I'm going to work on some home defences."

Bodin left the room and indeed, the world of the living, the bright red flash from the kitchen, confirming his departure.

"I'd like to see the bastards get past me!" Enkil half smiled.

CHAPTER 13

Emery and Jack had waited for an hour before calling Enkil to tell him the news. Enkil had seemed glad that something had finally started to go right for them. The news from his end wasn't entirely positive.

Bodin had brought a junior council member called Anders back through the portal with him to oversee the operation, but the consensus view of the council was to prepare for the worst. If Slarin's men were watching the place it was only a matter of time before they moved in.

"It's not safe for you to come back here, Emery," Enkil had said. "You're too important to risk getting killed in a fight, even though we're still not really sure as to why."

Emery had understood that, he wasn't particularly keen on being killed in a fight either. However, the next part of the council's plan hadn't exactly filled him with joy. He and Jack were to go back to Wormsley and Sons and secrete themselves until the place closed and then try to destroy the filing cabinet.

"How are we supposed to hide in a building full of people?" Emery had asked.

"You'll think of something," came the reply.

Emery had thanked Enkil for his 'help' and had then called a cab to go back into the city.

"So," said Jack as they clambered into the cab. "Where to first?"

"We need to stop at a hardware shop."

"A hardware shop?" Jack seemed mystified at the idea.

"Well, if we're going to destroy a filing cabinet, we'll need stuff to do it, won't we?"

"What kind of stuff did yi have in mind?"

Emery thought for a moment. "A hammer?"

The taxi pulled away from the cemetery and headed back towards the city.

"We'll need to get you a suit too, if you're going to get into the building. They'll never let you in looking like that."

"Aye, well that's fine by me. Ah did nay want ti put these back on anyway. Maybe it's because ah had that bath last night, but these clothes seem ti have a strange smell of piss aboot them that ah never truly noticed before."

Emery hadn't wanted to mention it but he had always been aware of the smell of piss and the smell of many more things besides.

The rain had started to abate, albeit only slightly, but Emery noted it none the less and chose to look upon it as an omen of good fortune. At the very least the clouds appeared lighter and that helped lighten his mood in some small way.

"So, you must know quite a lot about Hell then, what with you being able to speak with the dead and everything?"

"No, not really. Most of the people ah speak with are sort of in between."

"In between?"

"Aye, it's not always as clear cut as just one or the other. Sometimes people get stuck or attached here. It's complicated." Jack scratched his head. "For example, there was this one guy who caught his wife having an affair. Got in from work and there she was, bang at it with his best pal. 'Course, he was fucking livid, did his nut and hey presto, heart attack. Dead. Anyway, he chose to stick around and haunt the bitch."

"And you spoke to him?"

"Aye, just a chance passing really. Ah was cleaning oot the shitters one day and she went next door for a slash or something and ah picked up on him swearing at her. We ended up chatting, y' know."

Emery was hooked. It must be weird having the talent to casually chat with the dead. "So, you talked him into the light then?"

"Did ah bollocks! He was having a great time, the cheating bitch got what she deserved."

Emery was shocked. "But... what about his soul being at eternal rest and all that? Surely, it's not healthy to stay in limbo, clinging to petty revenge!"

"Not healthy? The man's dead. It can nay get any worse for him!"

"But, morally, shouldn't you have helped him cross over?"

"Well, ah never said ah was a priest. Besides, 'morally' shouldn't she have not shacked up with his best pal?"

Emery was lost for words.

"Ah rest my case. Anyway, it worked out for the best in the end. He met another girl in limbo, just like him and they crossed over together. Life's funny like that, eh?"

Emery shrugged. He hoped his life would have a happy ending.

*

Enkil had been busying himself with the business of safe-guarding the flat. If an attack was inevitable, he wasn't about to just sit there and wait for it to happen.

Since his death, twenty-eight years ago, he had quickly risen through the ranks to his current position working for the CNRH, mainly due to his fondness of self-defence. He seemed to possess a unique talent for the maiming of the enemy, a talent that had been heavily relied upon by the committee in recent months.

His first line of defence here would be the front door.

"Could you just pass me that axe?" Enkil asked Anders.

Anders nervously picked up the axe from an array of weapons laid out on the hallway floor and handed it to Enkil who was stood by the front door.

Anders had been here before on the night they had completed work on the portal. He had overseen the project and reported back to his superiors that all was well. Of course, that had been then and this was now and all was most certainly not well.

Anders had never been fond of conflict. He had been a nervous character in life and very little had changed him in death. His *life* career had been in the legal system where he had discovered that to make an even greater sum of money, all he had to do was take bribes, throw the odd case here and there and nobody got hurt. *But people did get hurt.* He hadn't been a party to any of the actual violence but he had played his part in the downfall of innocents just the same and for that he was condemned to Hell for a substantial amount of time. He couldn't grumble, he had steadily clawed his way to the rank of junior councillor and that was an achievement in itself. All in all, death had been relatively kind to him. Up until now that was. Now there was a war and that wasn't Anders' cup of tea at all.

"So, do you think an axe will be enough?" worried Anders, his voice quiet and trembling.

"I doubt it, but don't worry, I'll be putting plenty more 'tricks' around the place. They won't take the portal without losing a limb or two!"

Enkil tied the axe handle to the end of some rope,

which, via a varied network of pulleys, was attached to the door handle. He then drew the axe back, lining it up with the front door and taped the stem of it to the ceiling with thick gaffer tape.

"I hope one of the bastards tries to come this way!" Enkil chuckled.

Anders managed a nervous smile. "Okay, what's next?"

Enkil looked at the tools laid out on the carpet and allowed his eyes to wander over them. "Well, there's a couple of fire flares that I've been working on in the workshop. I suppose we could put one by the window in Emery's room and one by the back window in the lounge."

"Yes, that sounds comforting. We should definitely do that. What else?" Anders was chomping at the bit.

"One step at a time, mate." Enkil knew Anders was letting his nerves get the better of him and knew also that he wasn't doing any good hanging around, worrying himself to death. *Though clearly, he was already dead, (old sayings die hard).* "Go and have a beer or something."

Anders nodded and took the hint that he was probably getting under Enkil's feet. Perhaps it *was* better to just sit down with a beer. After all, he hadn't had one in nearly fifty years.

CHAPTER 14

It was almost half past four and the rain had eased to a drizzle. The clouds overhead, whilst remaining low and thick had lightened somewhat to a milder grey allowing something of the day to illuminate the busy city street, albeit slightly.

Jack vacated the taxi first.

Dressed in a dark grey suit, with white shirt and blue tie, he looked as most city businessmen looked and of course that was the idea. Emery had charged it all on his credit card. Normally he didn't like to do that sort of thing, but 'normally' had gone out of the window this week, along with 'usual sense of reality' and he wasn't sure when either of them were coming back. Besides which, he had unfortunately had no choice if he wanted the plan to succeed.

Emery stepped out of the cab and onto the pavement across the street from Wormsley and Sons. He carried a blue, canvas rucksack containing the tools he had bought from the hardware shop. He had originally thought to buy just a hammer but had then gone on to gather what would have amounted to a small toolbox worth of varied implements. He wanted to leave as little to chance as possible. He had then had to purchase a bag to put them all in, he couldn't after all be seen walking to his office with an armful of tools.

After 'arming' themselves and dressing Jack, they had stopped at a side street café and eaten full English breakfasts.

"We can nay go ti work on an empty stomach!" Jack had insisted. And he had been right, but it hadn't helped settle Emery's nerves any and now that he was face to face with the imposing building again his nerves began to take hold.

"Y' alreet there?" asked Jack.

"Yes… I'll be fine. I just…" Emery stammered to a pause, "I just can't believe what we're doing. It's crazy."

"Aye, it's nay sensible." Jack cut a mischievous grin. It seemed to Emery that Jack was quite enjoying the adventure of it all.

"Well, you seem alright with it," Emery blurted, envious of Jack's ability to soak up the pressure and get on with things.

"Aye, well that's because this isn't the worst thing ah've ever had ti do. Okay, the implications are a tad more severe, but the actual task itself? It's just a filing cabinet!"

"It's not just a filing cabinet though, is it?"

"Can we do this inside please, ahm getting piss wet through here!"

They waited a moment for a break in the traffic and then crossed the road into the shadow of the building.

"Well, here goes nothing!" Emery took a deep breath and then entered through the glass doors with Jack following closely behind him.

As the two walked through the lobby towards the reception desk, the receptionist looked up and stopped filing her nails.

Emery cursed under his breath. *Why?* Why was it that the one time he could really do *without* being noticed was the only time he did get noticed? *Bloody typical!*

"Ah, erm… hello. I forgot my bag earlier." Emery managed.

The woman looked at the rucksack draped over Emery's shoulder and then back up at him.

"Ah, no… not this bag. A different bag." He could feel beads of sweat running down his back. "Yeah, it's erm… a black bag. I've got a few of them. You know, different bags for different things." *Christ, could he dig himself in any deeper?*

Jack sensed the growing unease as the receptionist merely sat, staring.

"Listen," he butted in. "He forgot his shit, alreet? So, we're just gonna go up and get it, okay, Angela?"

Angela smiled. "Forgetful, eh?"

"Aye, he'd forget his own arse if he wasn't constantly sat on it!" Jack and the girl both laughed, Emery gave a nervous chortle and started to blush. "Reet, catch you later, princess."

With that the two walked from the reception area to the lift and entered. The doors closed and Emery breathed a huge sigh of relief.

"Princess?" he spurted.

"Aye." Jack brushed his hand through his rain-soaked hair. "Listen, ah had ti say something, didn't ah? Ah mean, what the Hell were you doing?"

"I was doing okay!" Emery protested.

"Okay at what? Is that how you normally talk ti women? *'Ah've got lots o' bags for different stuff'*?"

Emery pressed the button for the thirteenth floor. "Okay, okay, fair enough. I'm no good with women. We're in now anyway." He stood quietly for a moment as the first 'ping' sounded to mark their steady ascent. "How did you know what her name was?"

"How long have you worked here, Emery?" Jack scoffed.

Emery shrugged as the 'pings' continued to sound in the background.

"It's on her name badge. Reet there on her blouse," he tapped at his shirt. "You can't tell me you've never looked at her rack?"

"I never thought to. Can we just concentrate on what we're doing here, please?" Emery looked away from Jack to the digital display. *Sixth floor.*

"Okay, so where are we going then?" asked Jack.

"Thirteenth floor, that's where the filing cabinet is."

"Are we nay supposed ti hide for a bit first?"

That's when Emery realised his mistake.

Ping. *Seventh floor.*

"Oh, bollocks!" panicked Emery.

"What?"

103

"Oh bollocks! You're right! I just automatically pressed thirteen. I always do, it's habit!"

"It's okay, just don't get oot on thirteen. It'll stop and then we'll go back doon."

Ping. *Eighth floor.*

"What if we're seen? What if Hector sees me?" Emery put his head in his hands.

"What are the odds of that happening, eh?" Jack tried to console him.

'Get a grip, we'll be okay,' Emery said to himself.

Ping. *Ninth floor.*

And then the doors opened.

*

Enkil finished attaching the fire flare to the trip wire by the living room window and stood back from it to admire his work.

"That should do the trick," he said to himself. "Just remember not to stand too close to the windows," he added, looking at Anders who was sat nursing a beer on the settee.

"You know, I'd forgotten just how good beer was," Anders mused as he peeled the label from the bottle.

"And the doors, don't stand too close to the doors either."

Anders continued to stare at the bottle. "Why haven't we got beer down there?" he moaned.

"In fact, don't stand close to anything. Don't even stand actually, just sit there."

"Do you know what I mean though?" Anders turned to Enkil and held out his beer. "Why can't we get this in Hell?"

Enkil noted that Anders was perhaps a little merry and the slightest watermark of worry shimmered into the back of his mind. "How many have you had?"

"Only a couple," Anders protested. "Well, three. You did tell me to grab a beer, didn't you?"

"I did, yeah. I never told you to get shit-faced though."

"I'm fine." Anders placed the bottle onto the coffee table and sat back into the settee. "I've just not tasted anything that good in ages!"

"Well pace yourself, will you? We *are* expecting potentially violent company at some point this evening and unless your particular line of defence is puking, I imagine you'd prefer to be able to stand in order to make a run for it."

Anders got the point, though somewhat grudgingly.

"And the reason we don't have beer in Hell..." Enkil continued, "...is because beer's nice and Hell isn't. It wouldn't do for us all to be enjoying ourselves down there, would it? I mean that would sort of defeat the object of the place."

"Well, you say that but anyone who's ever had a hangover will tell you that *that* in itself is a form of Hell!"

"I think the council might contemplate allowing us the hangovers but I doubt they'll accept the beer idea."

Anders smiled. That's exactly what the council would do. He should know, he had worked alongside the committee for long enough now to know how their minds ticked.

Enkil picked up his satchel of tools and weapons. "Right, now for the last line of defence."

All this time, Bodin had been keeping watch on the parked car through Emery's bedroom window. Stood, arms folded, his tall, lean frame cut an imposing statuesque figure in the gloom of the room.

His patience and determination made him the ideal choice for recon work and the council had relied heavily on his attributes for centuries. Indeed, Satan himself had handpicked the demon to be one of his generals towards the end of his reign. Bodin wasn't given to sentiment or reflective musings, few demons were, but he found himself remembering those times now.

The good old days.

He referred to Satan's reign as such because there had been little or no paperwork, no bureaucracy and no red tape. If there had been any torturing or ferocious fighting to be done, it was simply done. And Bodin was good at both things. Particularly fighting.

As a demon in Hell, it was a necessity to become at home with the art of war. Of course, Bodin was no artist. There was little in the way of finesse about his fighting style. Barbarism, if it was an art form at all, was a very messy way of getting the job done. However, get the job done it did and Bodin's particular brand of barbarism had earned him the recognition and respect of the dark lord himself.

He had been busy slaughtering a breakaway tribe of malign demons when Satan had sent word of his promotion to General. For almost a century onwards he had held considerable power over his region of Hell and then came 'the great change'. Satan was denounced as Supreme Ruler and sent to live somewhere in the baron south realms and the committee took power shortly after.

Surprisingly, Satan hadn't put up a fight but merely accepted his fate. He had been busy with other projects towards the end of his reign anyway and Bodin supposed that he had regarded the situation as a sort of early retirement.

In the centuries that followed, torturing had become less commonplace and war had become almost non-existent. It wasn't the Hell that he had come to know and love. And so, his duties had changed, amounting to little more than that of a bodyguard to the suits he now worked for.

He couldn't complain, there were plenty worse off than him. And rightly so.

Bodin wasn't one for people, especially the types that ended up in Hell. They were usually maggots and worms, no strength of character at all. There was the odd one or two that deserved an iota of respect, Enkil being one of those. He had shown courage and conviction on numerous occasions, especially in the recent past and Bodin admired him for that. He was something of a kindred spirit in the way that he liked a good scrap, as the man had put it himself and that was something Bodin could connect with.

And that brought him back to the present.

The watchers in the car were still there, but he knew that it was only a matter of time before they made their move and he would be waiting for them when they did.

And he was looking forward to it.

CHAPTER 15

Emery stepped out of the lift first and into the empty corridor, looking around as he did so.

"How come it stopped on nine?" asked Jack also stepping out into the corridor.

"I don't know," Emery answered. "It's been doing that a lot recently."

They both scanned the doors that littered the walls of the corridor as the lift doors closed behind them.

"Well, I suppose we should pick a door then, eh?" suggested Jack.

"I suppose we should," Emery agreed.

They both walked a little way down the corridor and stood before a brown door before waiting for a moment.

"Are we going in or what?" asked Jack.

"What if there's someone in there?"

"Just tell them we've got the wrong room," Jack explained.

Emery nervously pushed the door open and slowly ventured his head around the corner. Not surprisingly for an office building, the room was in fact a small office with a regular sized wooden desk and a black leather-effect swivel chair. It was lit only by the stunted daylight stealing its way through a set of dusty blinds but Emery could clearly see that the room was free of people.

"Well?" prompted Jack.

"It's empty. I think we should be okay hiding in here for an hour or so until everyone finishes work." They both entered the room, Jack closing the door quietly behind him.

Emery put the blue bag onto the desk, relishing the relief of freeing the weight from his shoulder. He hadn't thought about the weight of the bag when he was buying the tools.

"Right, so we just wait here for an hour or so, yeah?" said Jack falling heavily into the chair and allowing it to swivel a little.

"Yeah," Emery chewed his lip in concerned contemplation, a nervous trait that manifested itself regularly.

"What's wrong?"

"Nothing. I mean, well... I'm just wondering why this floor's empty, that's all."

"Ah come on! You're thinking of things ti worry aboot. It's nay that strange by the way. Have you considered that maybe they do nay actually need every square inch of the building?"

"Well, yeah but it just seems a bit odd that it's set up like a working office." Emery opened one of the filing cabinets and began nosing through random files kept in there.

"Aye, well maybe it *was* a working office. Ahm telling you Emery, you've been watching too many films! Sometimes firms have cutbacks and maybe this was a part of the business they did nay need anymore."

Emery knew that Jack had a fair point but he couldn't ignore the nagging feeling lingering at his mind's fore. Something wasn't right here. He knew that something wasn't right with the building as a whole, specifically up on thirteen, but was it really mere coincidence that the lift had stuck on nine… again? He had obviously been relieved to a degree when it had; after all, he hadn't wanted to bump into Hector on thirteen. But it *was* weird that the lift had continued to stop on the ninth floor and if the last week had taught him anything, it was not to ignore the weird things. They all meant something, no matter how slight.

He closed the drawer to the filing cabinet and began to try the drawers in the desk, much to the annoyance of Jack who had to move his chair in order for Emery to do so.

"What are you looking for?" Jack enquired.

"I don't know yet," said Emery, frustrated at finding the drawers empty. "Are there any drawers next to you?"

Jack looked to his left, "No. Will you calm doon?

111

You're making me nervous and ahm nay given ti nerves!"

Emery had to concede that there was a distinct possibility that Jack was right. Maybe it was all this sneaking around that was taking its toll on him. Or maybe it was the week in general. A week ago, he would have scoffed at the very thought of trespassing on his employers' property. And furthermore, he was about to add 'criminal damage' to that list too by destroying the filing cabinet in his office.

He stood, back to the small window and slumped to the floor releasing a heavy sigh as he did so. He noticed a clock on the wall behind Jack.

4.58pm.

"Shouldn't be too much longer. Most people are normally out of their offices by ten-past." Emery said.

"What aboot the gaffers?" asked Jack.

"Gaffers?"

"Aye, gaffers. Y' know, the bosses."

"Oh," Emery thought for a second. "I don't actually know about them. I stayed a bit late one night finishing up an account and Little Worm left a bit before me. Maybe about half-past?"

"Right, well assuming that's normal behaviour..." Jack arched his neck over his left shoulder to look at the clock, "...we've a wee bit more than half an hour ti go before he's oot the way. What aboot the big man?"

"I don't know about him. Most of the time we never really knew whether he was here at all, although he probably was. Nobody really gets to see him very much, for all I know he could live here!"

"That does nay help us a great deal. We'll just have ti be quiet and hope for the best." Jack rubbed a hand through his hair and then began to take his tie off. "Ah never did like wearing a tie."

Emery gave out a small chuckle, "When did you ever wear a tie?"

"What, just 'cos ahm homeless ah've nay worn a tie before?" said Jack, feigning offence.

"When did you wear a tie?" repeated Emery.

"At school, smart arse." Emery laughed. "Or did you think ahd nay been ti school as well?"

It was growing darker outside now and the room was becoming stifled with shadow as a result.

"Do you think we should have checked the other rooms?" asked Emery.

"Ah think we'll be okay, ah mean we've nay heard anyone leaving in the corridor or anything."

Emery found himself looking at the clock again.

5.03pm.

"Yeah, you're probably right. We would have heard somebody by now. Most people like to be out of the offices by at least five-to-five, just to beat the rush for the lift."

The two sat in quiet for a moment, contemplating nothing in particular, simply waiting.

Emery spoke first.

"Do you think it will be easy to destroy the filing cabinet?"

"Ah reckon so, there's bound ti be something in the bag that'll do the trick, eh? You pretty much bought one of everything."

Emery smiled. It was strangely comforting that Jack

could remain cheerful throughout these testing moments. It made the stress somehow bearable.

No sooner than the thought had crossed Emery's mind, Jack's expression changed. Even in the fading light Emery could see his face turn a slate grey and his eyes take on an almost physical worry.

"Jack? What is it?" Emery was panicked now.

"Something's wrong." He stared at the desk, trying hard to focus on a single object to focus his mind.

"What? What's wrong Jack?"

"It's that sort of static fuzz again. The same as when we drove past that car on your street."

"Shit!" exclaimed Emery. "What does it mean?"

"Ah don't know but ahm thinking it's nay good. Ah think they know we're here."

Emery was startled out of words and struggled for a moment to say anything at all. "Shit!" he eventually settled on. "What shall we do?"

"Well ah don't think we should stay here." Jack stood from the chair almost at the same time that Emery leapt from the floor.

"Where to then?" asked Emery.

"You'd know better than me, ah've nay been here before! Think quick though, pal. The static's getting louder."

Emery grabbed the bag and hurried to the door, Jack following quickly after him. Upon opening the door, they crept cautiously into the corridor, which was now in virtual darkness.

"What happened ti the lights?" worried Jack.

"I suppose they must turn them off when everyone leaves," hoped Emery.

114

Their eyes darted feverishly around the darkness, desperately trying to focus on a way out and then the lift shaft hummed into life and the number thirteen lit up in red on the digital display above the lift doors, shattering the blackness around it.

The two stood as if rooted to the spot. Emery's breath seemed frozen to the roof of his mouth.

Ping. Twelve.

"Oh bollocks!" Emery yelped. "Now what?"

"Are there any stairs?"

"Er…" Emery desperately tried to think.

"For Christ's sake man, you must know where the stairs are!"

"Well, on twelve they're down that way," he said, pointing through the dark, some way past the lift.

"Right, let's get a move on then!" Jack pushed past Emery and scurried, whilst crouching, down the hallway. Emery followed him closely.

Ping. Eleven.

"Don't blame me if it's not this way!" wailed Emery.

"Ah will nay have time ti blame you, we'll both be dead!" Jack replied.

Within seconds they had made it to the end of the corridor where Jack felt around for a door.

"Is it there?"

Ping. Ten.

Jack smoothed his hands down the wall to his left and then hit upon a metal bar. He pushed down hard on it and the door opened onto an emergency stairwell, dimly lit by a single flickering fluorescent light at the bottom of a small flight of stairs.

"Quick, get in!"

Emery followed Jack onto the stairwell and closed the door behind him. He heard the 'last ping' sound out from the corridor as he did so.

"That was a bit too close for comfort," he whispered to Jack. "Now what?"

Jack scanned the steps leading down to the eighth floor and then looked up. "Well, we came here ti do a job, so let's go and do it, eh?"

"Won't it be too dangerous now?"

"We'll soon find out."

CHAPTER 16

Enkil was fitting a hetron capacitor to the fridge door when a small flash of red crackled behind him. He flinched a little and cursed under his breath as he nearly dropped the device he was holding.

"Shit!" he cursed. "That would have been the end of that plan if I'd have dropped that."

He turned around to see a smouldering note resting on the kitchen floor at the side of him. *What did the council want now?*

He picked up the note and scanned the scribbled writing.

ENEMY ADVANCING.
THE BRANG KALAG HAS BEEN FREED
AND IS UNDER CONTROL OF SLARIN!
WORSE NEWS-
IT'S NO LONGER IN HELL!

"Great!" Enkil blurted.

"What?" asked Anders, his head appearing through the doorway to the kitchen.

"As if we weren't in enough shit already! Slarin got to the Brang Kalag, it's under his control now."

Anders audibly gulped. "Oh dear. Do they need us back there to help?"

"No, because *it's* not there anymore."

"What do you mean, it's not there?"

"It's not in Hell. Which means it's here."

Anders seemed to grow even paler than his dead face already was. He had never actually seen the Brang Kalag, few had, but he had heard of it. A beast of such ill repute that everyone in Hell had heard of it and feared it. A soul destroyer.

One of Satan's early creations, it was made up of numerous demons, body parts and teeth. Lots of teeth. Too many teeth. A crazed creature that fed on the souls of the damned. *Here on Earth?* He could only imagine the carnage and it wasn't nice.

"Is it coming for us?" he worried.

"I don't know. But if it's not coming for us, it's going for Emery."

*

They had climbed the stairwell to the thirteenth floor and now both waited at the door that would hopefully lead to the corridor. They were quiet and crouching under the flickering fluorescent light.

"Can you hear anything?" whispered Emery.

"You tell me, you're closest ti the door," he replied quietly.

"I mean psychic stuff!"

"Ahm tryin' *not* ti listen for it, it's making me nervous," fidgeted Jack.

"Well, do you think you could give it a whirl, because I'd like a better idea of what's behind the door before I open it and get killed!"

"Aye, alreet, there's nay need ti get sarky!"

Jack squeezed his eyes closed and tried to concentrate. He cast his thoughts to the other side of the door, psychically trying to make his thoughts 'crouch down' so as not to disturb anything that might be on the other side.

"Ahm nay getting much."

"No static?"

"There's a wee bit but it seems a way off. Ah reckon it's doon on nine. Ahm nay getting anything through there."

Emery sat for a moment. "Shall we go in then?" he eventually said, knowing the answer anyway.

Jack nodded.

Emery reached up and pulled down on the bar as softly as he could and the door clicked open. He couldn't remember ever being as scared as he was now. He put that down to never having been as scared as he was now. *I mean, what experience could possibly hold a candle to this one?*

He crept into the dark corridor; Jack followed, keeping as low to the floor as possible and closing the door gently behind him. They appeared to be in an alcove of sorts and so Emery shuffled over to the corner of the wall, around which lay the long corridor leading to the door of special accounts.

"Anything there?" asked Jack.

Emery peeked around the corner. "No, it's empty."

They both scurried along the floor, squinting through the darkness to the end of the corridor. They seemed to go a little faster as they hurried by the closed lift doors on their right.

Upon reaching the door Emery reached up and gave the handle a pull, half expecting the door to be locked, but as he did so the door creaked open.

He peered into the office. The pillars of books and files were black silhouettes against the dull blue of the outside pressing against the window blinds behind them.

They both cautiously entered the room and closed the door behind them, the pair of them trying desperately to monitor even the volume of their breathing so as not to make a sound.

Jack nudged a stack of precariously stacked ledgers and the stack crumbled to the floor noisily causing them both to start.

"Shit!" Jack cursed.

Emery shot him a wide-eyed glance.

"Well, what the fuck? Who stacks books like this? Have you nay heard of shelves? And in case you have nay noticed, it's a wee bit dark in here, by the way!"

Emery sighed. "Why don't you wait here and I'll go and turn one of the small lamps on in the corner, since I know the layout."

"Aye, why don't you just do that? And while you're there, pick the place up a wee bit, it's like the arse end of Santa's fucking grotto in here."

Emery moved on through the dark, weaving his way through the obstacles and ignoring the comment from Jack.

As he reached Hector's desk, he grabbed the lamp from off it and placed it on the floor before switching it on at its base. The light was low and illuminated only the floor behind the desk to any great effect but caused shadows to sprawl menacingly throughout the office. The taller of the stacks of books cast the most far reaching of the shadows all the way over to the make shift kitchen area.

Jack crawled over to the desk to join Emery, who had already begun rifling through the drawers in the desk.

"What are you looking for?" asked Jack. "Where's the filing cabinet?"

"I'm looking for the ledger first."

"What ledger? You did nay mention a ledger! I don't know about you, pal, but I'd like ti get the job done and trot off, sharpish!"

"Look," Emery reasoned. "There aren't any clues in the cabinet, the files in there just disappear every night,

121

but every account we work on gets put in the ledger. It might help!" He continued to sort through paperwork and files that littered the drawers.

"Ah'll put the kettle on then, shall I?" said Jack sarcastically, whilst shaking his head. "Well ahm nay sitting here waiting around. Where's the filing cabinet? Ah'll make a start on it."

"In that room there." Emery pointed to it.
Jack shuffled off to the door in the corner and tried the handle. It was locked.

"It's locked!"

"I don't have a key. Hector must take it with him." He thought for a second. "We could try and pick it."

Almost before he could finish his sentence Jack kicked the door causing it to swing wildly open. Emery flinched at the noise.

"Jesus!"

"What?" asked Jack.

"I said pick it!"

"Ah thought you said kick it! Bollocks ti it anyway, ahm in!"

But that was where Jack stopped. An overwhelming sense of panic heaved into his mind.

"What's up?" asked Emery, noting Jacks inertia.

"Shite, we need ti get a move on. They're coming!"

Emery froze with fear. "Who… what… where?" he stuttered.

"It's nay static anymore, ah can actually hear them. Two Russian voices and… something else."

"Some*thing* else? What?"

"Ahm fucked if ah know and ah get the feeling that we're both fucked if we find oot!"

122

Emery began to rummage through the drawers even faster.

"Leave that for now, help me get something up against the door!" Jack leapt into action and ran over to the office entrance.

"I've got it!" yelped Emery, holding the ledger aloft.

"Great, give us a hand with this!"

Emery placed the ledger on the desktop and hurried over to Jack, who had begun to drag a rather heavy looking, fully laden set of shelves towards the door.

Emery took the other end and began to push, the shelves becoming only slightly easier to move, but they did so slowly and eventually they were in place, up against the door.

"What else?" Emery scoured for large objects in the dim light.

"Everything." Jack replied.

Emery spotted a filing cabinet behind several stacks of books near where the bookcase had been dragged from and pulled it from its place, setting it up against the shelves.

"That'll have ti do, they're getting too close!"

"Where are they, how long have we got?" Emery worried.

"They're on the stairwell. Grab the ledger and the bag, let's see ti the filing cabinet!"

Jack scurried to the door of the small office whilst Emery grabbed the ledger and the bag from off the desk. He reached around the desk and turned off the lamp before carefully side stepping more stacks of books on his way to join Jack. As he did so, they could both hear the sound of the stairwell door being slammed open at the far end of the corridor outside.

"Shit!" panicked Emery as he fled into the small office.

Jack reached up and pulled a large stack of wooden shelves down in front of the doorway that he stood in, the books falling heavily onto the floor as it fell. He then shut the door and looked around the office for something to put against the door.

Upon scanning the room he realised there was almost nothing in it. "For fuck's sake!"

"The desk!" said Emery, grabbing one end of it as he did so. Jack helped him and in an instant it was in place.

Breathing heavily, they waited and listened in the dark.

They weren't waiting long.

The dull rumble of charging feet from the corridor seemed to travel through the floor, rising up through their legs, feeling every step.

And then there was a colossal clatter as they hit the door to the main office.

Emery closed his eyes in a vain attempt to block out the situation but as he did so, an almighty roar erupted from the corridor. A deep, grating roar, as if ripped from the bowels of Hell itself. Of course, that wasn't too far from the truth.

"What was that?" Emery's panic had almost brought him to the brink of tears.

"Emery!" Jack shouted, "Snap out of it, pal! Get the bag open, we don't have long left!"

Emery did so to the increasing volume of pounding and snarling in the background.

It occurred to him then that these might be the last moments of his life and strangely his fear began to subside into anger.

He grabbed a hammer from the bag, gritted his teeth and repeatedly swung it at the filing cabinet.

Jack noticed the glint in his eye.

CHAPTER 17

It was half past five. Through the net curtains Bodin could still make out the car across the street. It was getting dark now, the early winter evenings had long started choking the daylight earlier each day but it was nothing Bodin's eyesight couldn't cope with.

In the dark of the room his eyes burned a deep red, his frame remaining steady along with his focus.

The street lamps outside flickered into life illuminating light waves of thin drizzle still falling through the air.

It wouldn't be long now, Bodin knew that they would make their move soon after the light had faded. They weren't waiting for darkness so as not to alert the neighbourhood to their presence, they didn't care about that. Their operation would be quick enough to avoid any unwanted police intrusion, not that they would particularly care about that either. The word 'covert' meant nothing to these fanatics.

No, they were waiting for darkness so as not to be seen coming by those they were coming for.

Bodin almost cracked a smile.

Slarin's men thought *they* had the advantage.

As Bodin watched, a black van rolled up and came to a halt behind the black car.

Two men stood from out of the car, one of them walked up to the van and leaned in through the passenger window.

So, this was it.

Bodin slowly moved away from the window and walked into the hall where Enkil spotted him from the kitchen.

"Is it on?"

Bodin nodded and grunted at the same time.

"Okay, mate. You stand at this entrance to the kitchen and watch the front door. Me and Anders will watch the living room side. If they get through the traps, we might be able to take out whoever's left. If not, you know plan B!"

Bodin grunted again. He wasn't one for plan B's. If anyone could get through *him,* they probably deserved a prize at the end of it.

"I know you don't care for plan B, but if they get through the portal, they'll be smack bang in the middle of the committee compound and if that happens, Slarin's pretty much won. So, we defend it while we can or we blow it up!"

Enkil knew he understood, he also knew that Bodin didn't much care for the committee himself, but defending it was a good excuse for a battle, a taste of the good old days when Satan was in charge. Of course, Enkil hadn't been there in 'the good old days' but he had heard about them often enough. *Often enough to know that 'the good old days' weren't actually that good at all.* No, Enkil would sooner have the committee in charge. It was far less messy.

"Anders, get in here!" Enkil shouted through to the living room.

"What is it? It's not time already, is it?" Anders had been on edge for hours, but his nerves tightened a few twists more as he stood in the doorway bridging the kitchen and the living room.

"It's time," Enkil confirmed. "All the traps are in place but in case a couple of the sneaky bastards get through we've got to be ready."

Anders felt sick but nodded his understanding.

"You and me here watching the room, Bodin there watching the hallway."

They were in position, now all they had to do was wait.

Enkil and Anders were crouched down now; the only light in the kitchen apart from the shimmering red glow emanating from the crack in the floor was the flickering light being cast out from the television in the living room. All lights in the apartment had been turned off one by one as Enkil had completed each of the traps.

Bodin remained standing, arms folded. His red eyes glared at the front door at the end of the hallway with such an intensity that he could have almost burned through it.

All three of them were silent, their eyes fixed on the entry points before them. The only noise was that from a cartoon on the television, which was spewing forth all manner of comical noises that were inappropriate for the mood.

"I wish you'd have turned the bloody television off!" Enkil said to Anders.

"Do you want me to?"

"Nah, leave it," he sighed.

They were silent again for a moment, watching intently.

"Maybe they'll go to the wrong house," offered Anders.

"Yeah, and maybe we'll all go to Heaven after this and be allowed to drink beer without the hangover!" Enkil gave a half smile. "I think if we had that kind of luck, we wouldn't have gone to Hell in the first place, eh?"

Anders tried to smile through the worry but his face couldn't quite manage it.

"Still, it's a thought though, isn't it?"

And then they heard a pane of glass break, as if tapped by a small hammer.

"The bedroom," whispered Enkil. "It's started."

*

Emery took the hammer to the filing cabinet like a man possessed, smashing and battering its sides. Jack didn't know whether to be impressed at his enthusiasm or scared by it. There was something unnerving about the look in Emery's eyes, almost as if he wasn't there any more.

The truth was of course that he was there. No one had possessed him at all.

It's strange the way terror can take a man. Some panic and crumble, some panic and run. But some simply stop panicking and cope and the way they cope is by tapping into some hitherto unknown reserve of strength or madness that might somehow see them through the situation.

It wasn't planned, it wasn't even understood. Emery simply didn't care any more.

The truth was that at the end of a week like this one, Emery didn't have any other answers and so it was almost like autopilot had kicked in. He was barely in the driving seat at all at this point and it felt good.

He felt much better this way and it was anger that was driving him now.

Anger at his predicament, anger at the people or *things* chasing him, anger at the enemy and anger at Hell itself. After all, what had he done in life to deserve any involvement with Hell at all? Nothing, *that was what.* And now he was dragged into all this mess!

He had lived a life of no significance to Hell or anything else. Safe. There was safety in numbers, *wasn't that what his grandad had told him?* He perhaps hadn't meant it quite so literally.

The thoughts scampered dizzily through his mind as he wailed the hammer into the cabinet, denting the thin metal with satisfying clatters.

Jack reached into the rucksack and pulled out a small bottle of fire lighting liquid.

"That'll do the trick!"

He quickly twisted the top off and squeezed its contents all over the cabinet, the fumes immediately assaulting his nostrils.

Emery threw the hammer to the floor and yanked the top drawer from its housing until its runners stopped it in its tracks.

"Shit!" he yelled, using every sinew to pull at the drawer.

"Emery, stand back! Ahm aboot ti set it off!" shouted Jack.

Emery paused, his breathing calming to allow in other sounds. But the sounds were ones from the corridor and they weren't pleasant. Growls, snarls, kicking and pounding.

Within moments they would be through that first door, Emery had little doubt. *And then what?* There was only a table and a bookshelf in the way of this door!

And then they heard it, the crashing of the main door finally giving in to the onslaught from the corridor and with that noise came a horrible realisation that now only one door would stand in the way of them and death.

Jack struck a match from his pocket and tossed it into the open drawer of the filing cabinet. Instantly, flames erupted into life and leapt upwards, blistering the paintwork on the ceiling.

"Is that it?" coughed Emery through the plumes of black smoke bellowing through the room. "Is it destroyed?"

"It looks pretty knackered ti me!" spat Jack through the flickering heat of the flames.

Emery looked around him for a moment, as if only just taking note of his surroundings. "Now what?"

"Well, ahm up for leaving."

"How?" Emery motioned to the door with the desk up against it.

"The window?"

"Thirteen floors up, Jack!" Emery reminded him. "And I can't fly."

"Ahm open ti suggestions then but as ah see it, the only other option's the wall and ah can nay walk through walls!"

The two stood staring at each other and then frantically began to look around for an exit strategy. There seemed little or no hope of finding one.

"Well, we could do with getting back ti the stairwell or the lift, that's our only way oot!" Jack rushed the thought through his head to his mouth without stopping to mull it over.

"Well yeah. The problem's getting out of this room though, isn't it? I'd rather not go that way," he said pointing at the door. "It sounds a bit dangerous."

"Well, we're running oot of options, pal. If we don't think of something quick, we'll both burn ti death!"

The bookshelf behind the door crunched into life, scraping the door as it moved.

"Shit!" panicked Emery.

They both looked towards the window

CHAPTER 18

There was a handful of seconds quiet and then an explosion. The floor shook and Bodin noticed a wave of smoke drift from under the bedroom door.

"That's the bedroom gone then," said Enkil, crouching next to the cooker in the kitchen. Anders was next to him, trembling.

As it fell silent again, they could hear a car alarm sounding off on the street outside.

"The neighbours will be complaining about this for years," Enkil managed to muster a small smile. It disappeared just as quickly as it came.

Bodin noticed the door handle twisting on the front door and he smiled cruelly and unfolded his arms.

The handle stopped moving and then the door immediately burst open, swinging wildly and almost taking its hinges with it. There was a figure dressed in black standing the with a machete that reflected the streetlamps. He caught a glimpse of Bodin, standing tall, eyes burning, with a wide mocking smile growling at him.

Bodin recognised the look on the man's face as fear. That was just before the axe swung down from the ceiling in the hallway and buried itself into the man's face.

His body stayed upright for a few seconds longer, blood gushing from the wound and then he fell limply to the floor, his eyes still wide with terror and surprise.

There were movements out on the street. It was scattered though and Bodin couldn't make out fully what was happening but within an instant he knew something was wrong.

Enkil somehow sensed it too and he looked from the living room window to the hallway. Of course, he couldn't see the door clearly as it was obscured by Bodin's ample frame but from his crouching position he saw the grenade roll into the hallway and he shouted. He wasn't sure if he was actually shouting a word or not but he knew he was sending a signal from his brain to his throat. What actually came out was a garbled noise.

Bodin had already seen the grenade and reached down and picked it up. He squinted his eyes; the burning red venom now just slits in the gloom of the hall. He focused on the black van across the street that had brought these so-called soldiers and launched the grenade back out of the house.

It smashed through the passenger window where a

startled looking man sat. He immediately dropped the radio he was holding and scrambled around looking for the door handle.

The explosion was huge, illuminating the whole street for a split second and covering it in metal shards and chunks of dead men in the next.

"Jesus!" shouted Enkil. "Good shot!"

Suddenly Anders shouted.

"Enkil! Living room!"

Enkil turned his attention to the living room window. There were shadows moving behind it, seemingly closing in on the window.

"You might want to cover your ears!" said Enkil.

They both did so and a moment later the window exploded showering the living room with glass. Smoke clung to the air strangling the silence from every particle.

Through the open front door Bodin could see what looked like a platoon of soldiers wearing black amassing on the lawn. *There must have been more than one van.* All of a sudden, he wasn't so sure as to who had the upper hand any more. 'Pride comes before a fall' someone had arrogantly once told him. He couldn't quite remember who but he never saw the man again. Apparently rebels slaughtered him.

Enkil saw it too and heard footsteps from the back yard.

He looked at Anders who still had his hands on his ears.

"Well, this looks bad," he said quietly.

Bodin turned his head and grunted slightly.

"We might have to resort to plan B after all." Enkil

stared at the device over his left shoulder.

Bodin returned his gaze to the hallway only to be met by a tall figure in a long, black coat staring back at him. His hair was short and white and his eyes were like deep black caverns surrounded by a slate grey rock face. He was looking past Bodin to the crack in the kitchen floor.

Slarin.

*

Emery was stood on the windowsill having ripped the blinds from their moorings in the wall. He desperately searched for an opening mechanism but couldn't find one.

"Hurry up!" shouted Jack who was stood beneath him.

"I'm trying!" Emery yelled back. "There's no handle, it's a sealed window!"

The movements behind the door were sounding more erratic now, the trashing of the obstacles against it all but finished and the noise of whatever beast lay beyond roaring through the doorframe.

Jack looked around and noticed the chair in the corner of the room.

"Emery!" he shouted as he reached and grabbed it. "Move oot the way!"

He held the chair above his head as Emery jumped down from the windowsill, careful to avoid the filing cabinet, which was now a raging inferno.

He threw the chair as hard as he could but the window refused to give way; the chair sent bouncing off back to the corner of the room.

"Bastard!" Jack shouted, reaching for the chair again to give it another go.

Too late.

The door burst open sending shards of wood splintering through the air. Through the billowing black smoke wafting towards the doorway, they could both make out a seven-foot mass of sinew and teeth standing there growling.

Words couldn't express the kind of fear that they both felt. Even fear was having a hard time expressing just how terrifying the beast was.

It turned its attention towards Jack who had the chair held above his head and then to Emery, who was stood, petrified to the core behind him.

The moment seemed to last forever. The looks between them, an eternity. Emery felt useless. *This was it, his time was up. So long job, so long apartment, so long life!*

And then, shattering the moment back into action, Jack hurled the chair at the beast, hitting it in the face and sending it reeling backwards a few steps.

"Now!" shouted Jack. He grabbed Emery by the shirt collar and pulled him towards the door in a vain attempt to dummy the flailing beast and make a bolt for freedom.

The beast recovered quickly though and charged back

into the room, its rage screaming through its face, each piercing cry sharpening itself on razor sharp teeth as it raced into the room.

As it did so it knocked Jack backwards into the burning filing cabinet, he in turn yanking Emery along with him.

"Argh!" They both wailed as they fell into the flames.

And then something strange happened.

As soon as they hit the metal of the disintegrating cabinet, there was a flash of red. It filled the room, merging with the fire and the screams of the creature.

And then there was red everywhere.

Emery squinted through the flames and then everything whistled into nothingness.

He tried to turn his head to see Jack but found himself paralysed. Staring into the dark, he screamed but heard nothing.

An enormous pressure seemed to be building up inside his head as if he were in a plane during a steep descent and he started to shake uncontrollably. *What was happening to him?*

It lasted no more than ten seconds before wind started rushing up past his face and then he knew he was falling. Fast.

Air slowly appeared back in his lungs and he almost choked on his own screams as they burst out of him into the darkness.

All of a sudden, he felt swamped by the most enormous swell of potential energy, fizzing and crackling around him and then he was motionless again.

The darkness seemed to be taking on grey forms, blinking into existence around him like static on a television, swirling and crunching into being but taking on no recognisable shape.

And then there was a huge bang as he was spat out of the darkness and on to something hard and very real, smouldering and singed from flame.

He lay there, trembling, too scared to move or even open his eyes.

What the Hell was that? What had happened?

Emery assumed that he hadn't burned to death. Not that he knew what burning to death felt like, but he assumed it would have been hotter. He hadn't felt hot at all, in fact there had been almost no sensory feeling.

There was *now* of course. He ached, as if he had been caught under a stampede of elephants.

He took in a breath of stale air and slowly shock receded into resignation.

He knew full well where he was and he knew what had happened. But he daren't open his eyes. *How could he open his eyes and acknowledge his worst nightmare?*

There was a build up of static electricity to his left and this brought on an excruciating case of pins and needles. He grimaced at the discomfort before flinching at the small explosion next to him.

Something fell to the ground with a thump.

After a deep inhaling of stagnant air, it spoke. "Ah think ah've shat ma' self!"

CHAPTER 19

Enkil and Anders stood from their crouching positions realising that they were surrounded. Enkil looked at the hetron device attached to the fridge door and wondered if he could make it there before being taken down. He looked back at the figure now staring straight into Bodin's eyes.

Slarin stood, unflinching, his black eyes staring coldly into Bodin's.

"You would do well to move, demon." His voice was low and in a pronounced Russian accent. "I won't tell you again."

Bodin grunted and turned and stood with his colleagues.

Slarin looked them up and down with disdain. "I

demand your full co-operation. This is not a request understand, you have no choice but to obey me."

Enkil cursed himself. *How had this happened?* He had felt so sure that the traps would have seen off the enemy.

"Where in Hell does the portal lead?" Slarin asked.

All three remained defiantly silent.

"You should save yourselves time and tell me now, because ultimately you will tell me, I can promise you this. And if I have to wait for my answer, you will be telling it to me through tears of pain."

"Give us a bit of credit, mate," said Enkil. "You're trying to intimidate people who've been in Hell a lot longer than you."

Slarin stared at him.

"You've been in Hell for two minutes and you think you're the dog's bollocks!" Enkil continued. "Well, you're not. We've seen shit that would make you cry like a little girl, so don't come in here swinging it like you're the big one 'cos we're not impressed."

Bodin almost smiled. He liked that about Enkil. He was the sort of person who would have even told Satan where to get off. Sheer grit.

Anders was cringing however at the thought that Enkil was possibly making a very bad situation much worse.

Slarin smiled a sickly smile, his eyes darkening though by the second.

"It is good that you have sense of humour, I look forward to making you choke on it. And as for the 'shit you've seen', I assure you when Hell finally falls to my will, I will create new agonies for each of you."

"Well, make sure you get more creative with it than

what you are with your little speeches 'cos frankly, mate, I'm embarrassed for you."

Enkil smiled at him.

"You have cocky mouth, soldier," Slarin started. "But to quote one of your English phrases, how you say, 'he who laughs is longest but will laugh last out loud.'"

Enkil looked bemused. "You haven't got a clue have you?"

A split second later he was hit around the head with the butt of a machine gun and he crumpled to the floor, unconscious.

*

Emery and Jack picked themselves up from the floor and looked around them. They were in a small room lit only by two flaming torches mounted on the stone walls. The architecture was basic to say the least. There were no features to speak of apart from a wooden door set into one of the walls. It had a small, square window hollowed into it with four iron bars sat vertically through it.

"Are we where I think we are?" asked Emery, turning his gaze towards Jack.

"Shit Creek, you mean? Aye, ah reckon we just might be." Jack walked cautiously up to the door and peered through the window.

142

"Anything?"

"Just a corridor." He pulled on the iron handle on the door and with a heavy moan it opened. "You up for a wander?"

"A wander?" Emery was shocked. "Are you kidding? Do you know where we are?" He didn't even dare say it out loud.

"Aye, ah know where we are but unless you want ti wait around for that fucking mouth on legs ti follow us doon here, ah reckon we ought ti get a move on!"

Emery thought for a second. *They were in Hell*, of that he was certain. Was it really a good idea to start nosing around the place? Probably not, but then again, was it really a good idea to wait where they were on the off chance that the beast was on its way there too? Now was no time for ambivalence.

Just as the thought of leaving occurred to him, Emery noticed the air fill with static and a second later the mouth on legs exploded into being and hit the floor with a huge thump.

"Shit!" he exclaimed, running towards the door.

The creature was stunned and still smouldering from the fire back at the office.

Jack ran up to the beast and began kicking it with every ounce of strength he could muster.

Emery joined him, after grabbing one of the flaming torches from off the wall. He wasted no time in setting light to the wailing monster and then stood back and watched as the burning mess writhed and then eventually twitched to a charred stop.

"Let's not hang aboot for the soldiers though, eh?" Jack said through heavy breaths.

143

Emery nodded and they both hurried over to the door where they began to make their way down the corridor.

The corridor was narrow and made from the same grey stone as the room. Emery guessed that it ran for about fifty metres before splitting into a T-junction.

"Which way?" he asked Jack, upon reaching the end.

Jack looked both ways. To the left there lay another corridor that appeared to be a similar length to the one they were in, to the right there were steps spiralling downwards and to the left.

"Ah think we should take the steps."

"Why?"

Jack seemed lost for a reason. "Because it looks different? Ah don't know why, ah mean we can flip a coin if you prefer!"

"Alright, alright, I was only asking."

As they descended Emery noticed that the temperature was rising. He wiped the sweat from his forehead with the back of his hand, still holding the ledger tightly. It didn't take long before they reached the foot of the staircase, which opened out on to what looked like a row of ten or twelve cells. They were small stone walled rooms with barred doors enabling them to see through to the cells within. Shadows of people lurked there.

"Shit," said Emery. "Perhaps we should go back."

"Nah, ah say we chance it. Someone doon here might know how ti get oot."

"I think you're being slightly optimistic. If they knew a way out do you honestly think they'd still be locked up?"

Jack realised Emery had a point but he pushed on regardless.

"They might know something aboot the place that could help us," he concluded.

To the left of them, they rounded the first cell. In it sat an almost naked man, probably somewhere in his mid forties, in manacles chained to the wall. He was covered in dirt and looked mildly distressed to say the least.

"Y'alreet, pal?" said Jack.

The man responded with mild panic, turning away and scrunching eyes closed.

"It's alreet, pal, ahm nay here ti hurt you. Me and my pal here are a wee bit lost, you could nay help us oot, could you?"

The man turned his head to face them and looked the two over. "What's it worth?"

Jack was a little taken back at the reply. "Er, we have nay really got anything," he thought for a second. "You can have my jacket if you like."

"What am I going to do with a jacket? It's boiling in here!"

Jack and Emery didn't know how to respond and for a moment there was an awkward silence between them.

"Well, what do you want?" asked Emery, eventually.

"I want to get out."

"What are you in for?" asked Jack.

"I'm a dentist."

"Ah say we leave the bastard there," said Jack. "Let's try the next one." With that, they both left the man and walked slowly along the row of cells.

The next two cells were empty and the one after had a hideously huge man in it, who stared at them and smiled through the bars. It was an unnerving smile to say the least. Emery and Jack shared a knowing glance to each

145

other, which basically meant 'I'm not asking this one for anything' and moved along to the next one.

The next cell was larger and darker than the others and Emery's eyes had to strain through the shadow to make out two figures sat, slumped against the back wall.

"Hello?" said Emery, into the darkness.

"Emery?" came the reply. The figure stood up and stepped out of the shadows.

"Enkil?"

"Emery, Jack, how did you get here?" Enkil asked, as Bodin stood and joined him.

"It's a long story but we sort of went through the filing cabinet, we think."

"I said destroy it not climb into it," Enkil remarked.

"We did nay have much time ti think aboot it, we got knocked in there by an ten-foot ball of teeth!" said Jack bitterly.

"Yeah, the Brang Kalag, we heard about that getting out, sorry."

"Aye, well it's a crispy fried Kalag noo and if it's any consolation ah think the cabinet's pretty much on its arse as well."

"What are you doing in here?" asked Emery.

"Slarin got the better of us back at the flat, took us through the portal and locked us up in here until he takes over the compound. Then I imagine he'll torture us for a while."

Emery handed him the ledger through the bars of the cell. "I got this from work, it might be of help. Hector and my boss must be in on it."

Enkil opened the ledger to the last page with writing

on and scanned down the entries. His finger rested on one entry in particular.

AL 3,345 SLARIN, IGOR

"That's the one. Hectors signed his name next to it so you could be right," said Enkil. He closed the ledger and handed it to Bodin. "We also know that there was a man on the inside here, working in points division. Anders."

Bodin grunted his anger at the mere mention of his name.

"He told Slarin that the portal led to the compound too, that's why we're back here."

"What do we do about Hector and Big Worm?" asked Emery.

"I wouldn't worry about them, they'll be down here soon enough and with the cabinet out of the way they can't do any more damage anyway. No, the problem we've got now is Slarin. We can't let him take over the compound or Hell's his!"

"What do you want us ti do?" asked Jack.

"First things first, get us out of here and then I'll tell you the plan."

"How? If anyone was going ti rip the bloody bars open it's probably the fella you have in there with you!"

"There should be some keys on the wall at the end of

the row. That's where they usually are, I've been down here quite a few times."

Emery looked towards the end of the row of cells and sure enough, there was a bundle of keys hanging from a rusty hook in the wall.

A minute later and the cell was open.

"That was surprisingly straight-forward," said Emery.

"Aye, they might want ti rethink where they hang those," added Jack.

"Right," said Enkil, "Let's get it on!"

CHAPTER 20

"Slarin and his men will be in the higher echelons of the compound. They will have made straight for the committee chambers to seize power. That's where the true running of Hell takes place."

"So, that's where we've got to go then?" asked Emery.

They had left the holding cells and made their way back up the staircase and into the corridor that Emery and Jack had walked through earlier. From there they had made their way down several more staircases prompting Emery to wonder just how deep the compound went. He shrugged his thoughts off however, by fully acknowledging that he was after all in 'Hell' and that in itself must have been quite deep.

They had come to a stone door set a little aside from one of the many stone corridors that they had travelled and Enkil had begun dictating his plan.

"No, we should avoid the chambers completely."

Emery's face grew puzzled.

"I'll explain. The compound has an internal security system, a sort of last resort. Everyone who works or resides in the compound has a device implanted in them that creates a sort of shield around them."

"A kind of force field?" Jack interrupted.

"No. It's… more a type of pulse signal. It actually emits a kind of radiation that's monitored at all times. When the system is triggered anyone without the implant is, how can I put it, incapacitated?"

"Incapacitated? That's a bit vague, isn't it?" said Emery, frowning at Enkil's ambiguity.

"It's a molecular reshuffle, very messy."

"So, we just trigger the device then?" asked Jack.

"It's not quite as easy as that."

"Why am I not surprised at that?" Emery put his head in his hands. "What's the catch?"

"Well, firstly it's behind that stone door. It's sealed. I mean, it wouldn't do to be able to just stroll in and switch it on, would it? There could be foreign dignitaries visiting."

"Foreign dignitaries? From where? This is Hell!" Emery's bafflement was growing into disbelief.

"Yes, but Hell is a republic now and ever since the committee took power, we get the occasional visit from goodwill ambassadors from 'upstairs'. They come to collect the redeemed."

Emery nodded his understanding. "Of course, they do," he added dryly.

"Well, that sort of leads me to the second thing. You

two aren't supposed to be here. If we set it off you will be…" Enkil paused to structure his words tactfully, "...incapacitated."

All of a sudden, the reality of the situation, *which had incidentally been missing for most of the week,* hit Emery like a lead weight.

"Oh," he managed. "Isn't there anything else we can do?"

"I'm afraid not."

There was silence for a short while, both Emery and Jack having nothing to say and Enkil not wanting to say anything. But it was Enkil who broke the silence.

"I'm sorry guys, but we have to do this and we don't have much time. The way I see it, your only chance is to make it to the portal room, jump through and get back to your flat. Once I've set the device off, the portal will automatically break down."

Emery immediately felt a ray of hope shine upon him. "Yes! That's a good plan, how do we get there?"

"It's the next floor down, take the next left," he began, using his hands to aid the instructions, "take the staircase down, along the corridor and then go through the door marked 'Do Not Enter'."

"Wouldn't it be easier if you just showed us the way?" asked Emery.

"I don't have time, it's going to take me *and* Bodin to get this door open, I've got to set the device off before all control of Hell is relinquished to Slarin. If that happens, it'll be too late for even this to work!"

Emery took a deep breath. And then another one for good measure.

"Better get going," said Jack urging Emery on.

Emery looked at Bodin, who merely grunted slightly. He wasn't one for sentiment.

"Good luck, Emery," said Enkil.

"Yeah, you too." For some reason that Emery couldn't readily understand, he felt that he was going to miss Enkil. "Try not to get yourself killed," he added.

"Well, I'm already dead, but thanks. You better get going. You've got about five minutes."

Emery and Jack started to make their way down the corridor towards the stairs.

"Oh, and Emery," shouted Enkil. "Thanks. You too, Jack."

"Any time," said Jack. Emery nodded.

"And I'm sorry about your flat," Enkil added, then turned to help Bodin with the stone door.

Emery smiled and looked at Jack. "It's just a crack in the floor, the landlord thinks it's subsidence. It'll be fine."

They began to run down the corridor and onto the stairs that met them.

*

The committee chambers were much more elaborate than the rest of the compound. Its ornately patterned ceiling sat on huge granite pillars, which in turn were adorned in a crimson and gold scrollwork.

A huge stone table lay in the middle of the hall, large enough to seat the twenty members of the committee. On the table were several tall, golden torches, their flames reaching high into the air, illuminating most of the room.

The committee members sat around the table now, surrounded by almost fifty armed, dead Russians. Their pallid and gaunt features flickered eerily in the firelight.

Slarin's dead eyes betrayed little emotion as he stared at the council before him. He slowly walked towards the table, surveying each member as he did so.

"Slarin, you can't believe this insanity will work!" spoke one of the council.

"But it has worked. I'm here, aren't I?" A smile crept onto his face. "Don't think of it as end of era..." he said in that monotone and broken English "...think of it as beginning of new one. A better one, with no debates, no forums, no votes and no arguments. That was problem on Earth, everybody talk and nothing get done. Well, it is my time now!" The council members looked on as Slarin prattled on, his megalomania getting the better of him.

"I find it disturbing that the 'almighty Satan' stood aside for such pitiful excuse for rulers. Was he, how you say, big girl's blouse? Just handing it over without a fight?"

"Satan stood down because it was his time," came a shout from the table. "He did it for the good of Hell. Progress."

"Progress?" Slarin laughed, mockingly. "How is it progress? You have almost done away with torture, you call this progress? This is Hell, people expect torture!

153

You should be investing in new and improved forms of torment and depravity for the scum that ends up here! To coin phrase, how you say, 'make hay when grass is green.'"

The committee sat in uncomfortable silence, occasionally looking at each other with beaten expressions.

"Well, now is the time for change. You will join me comrades, join me or waste away in cells of anguish and despair. Personally, I hope you don't join me. I look forward to eating your intestines while my minions piss in your eyes."

Some of the council members' faces were beginning to portray mild disbelief. *What was this guy on? Eating intestines whilst pissing in their eyes?* He was clearly mad.

"And now gentlemen, I will have the codes to your systems to ensure a smooth transfer of power."

There was a wall of quiet, broken only by the occasional stifled cough.

"For every minute that nobody speaks, one of you will perish, yes?"

The soldiers raised their guns and pointed them at those seated around the table, whilst Slarin folded his arms and waited.

CHAPTER 21

Emery and Jack were both out of breath. They had run through a multitude of different corridors and were currently lost.

"It's doon here, ahm sure of it," wheezed Jack, propping himself up against a wall to get his breath back.

"I'm sure we've been down here already." Emery too leaned against the wall.

"How can you tell, Emery? They all look the same ti me."

"I've just got a bad feeling, call it a hunch. It's been that kind of week."

The two rested for a moment longer before setting off again down the corridor. As they drew to the end they veered left only to draw back into the corridor, sharply.

"What?" whispered Emery.

"There's a guard there! Enkil did nay say anything aboot guards!" Jacks voice was low but frustrated.

"How many?"

"Two."

Emery thought for a second. "Let's think of a plan."

"We have nay got time for a plan! Need ah remind you that in aboot three minutes me and you are going to be demolecule... ised!"

"Incapacitated," Emery corrected him.

"Whatever it is! Is that how you want ti be remembered? A big old red stain on that wall?"

"Alright then braniac, hat do you suggest?"

"Let's just get 'em."

"Just get them? That's your big idea?" Emery shook his head.

"Aye. You want ti go and talk them round ah suppose?"

"We could try it at least."

Jack now shook his head. "Ok, we'll try it your way first, but it's nay just your own time your wasting, pal. Remember that. Ahm gonna be a stain on a wall as well, so hurry it along, would you?"

With that, Emery took a deep breath and walked confidently from out of the corridor, Jack following behind him. The two guards saw them and held their staffs defensively across the door.

"Who goes there?" demanded one of them in a gruff voice.

"Hello there," Emery began. "We are from committee support, here to inspect the room."

"No-one goes in, orders from the top." The two stared at Emery blankly.

"These are new orders. I'm giving them to you now."

"On whose authority?"

Emery was trying desperately to sound convincing but hadn't had much practice in the art of deception and was beginning to crack under the pressure.

"Er... the top authority. It's from the top, so... step aside soldier and let's have a bit less lip." He was twitching now with nervousness.

The soldier cracked a scowl. "No-one goes in and that's the last time I'm telling you."

Something in Emery snapped, similar to what happened back at Wormsley and Sons. He was swept with impatience and frustration, grabbing the guard by the chest of his grey uniform and pushing him up against the wall.

"Listen here you thick bastard! The compound is overrun with Slarin's men and we need to get into that room." Emery was shaking now, as the adrenaline coursed through him. "Now, one way or another we're going in and if that means we've got to go through you, then bring it on!"

Jack looked on with mild amusement, whilst keeping a close eye on the other guard who had raised his staff and was poised, ready to join in.

"Now what's it going to be?"

*

Bodin and Enkil had spent the last few minutes pushing the stone door. At first, they had made very little progress but Bodin had eventually let rip with his frustration and that had seemingly doubled his already ample strength. It had still taken them both to move it but once they had found momentum the door slid steadily backwards, grinding noisily into the wall behind it.

The narrow corridor that led on from there was dark and oddly cold.

"I can't see a thing," moaned Enkil, leading the way.

Bodin grunted in agreement as he followed, brushing dust webs from out of his face as he went.

As they entered something of a wider area, a torch mounted on the wall ahead of them burst into flame and lit their surroundings.

The room was unsurprisingly made of stone, the same grey stone that ran through the whole compound. There was a stone altar in front of them with a ruby chalice resting upon it.

Enkil looked around to see if there was anything else. *Switches, levers, buttons, anything.*

There was nothing.

He looked at Bodin and then back to the altar, baffled.

"This can't be it, surely! Where's the device?"

He walked to the altar and peered into the chalice. There was a liquid in it, of that much he was certain, but how could that possibly be relevant?

He walked around the altar to see if there were any devices hidden from immediate view. There was nothing.

Bodin grunted and nodded to the chalice.

"You think this is it?" asked Enkil.

Bodin nodded and motioned for Enkil to drink from it.

"You want me to drink from it? It could be anything in there!"

And then, for the first time, to Enkil's ears at least, Bodin spoke.

"It is the blood of Satan. Drink from the chalice and his power will be released through you."

"Okay, didn't know you could talk, so that's new for one thing and for another, I'm not really keen on drinking the blood of Satan. You do it."

"I am *from* Hell, it has to be one who has *come to* this place. It has to be you."

Enkil looked with disgust at the chalice. Drinking blood was simply something that held no appeal for him, especially the blood of Satan himself.

'Ok. Just pretend it's a beer,' he said to himself.

He picked up the chalice with his right hand and sniffed tentatively at it. Pungent didn't even begin to describe it. He pulled his nose away quickly.

"Christ," he grumbleded. "I'm going to have trouble keeping this down."

*

The shot from the gun echoed throughout the tall chambers.

"That really hurt!" protested the council member. As he sat upright again, the side of his face hung limply onto his shoulder. Blood pulsed from the wound, spraying the table in thick, red puddles.

The others looked on in terror.

"I told you that I am not a man of patience. Perhaps now you believe me." Slarin chuckled to himself. "It is like the saying, 'patience is a virgin I am not possessing.'"

"That's enough!" A bearded man with a tall, black hat stood abruptly from his chair. "You can have the codes! Please, just no more sayings!"

Slarin laughed loudly. "I did not think you would break so easily!"

As the council member slumped dejectedly back into his seat, the walls began to shake.

"What is happening?" Slarin shouted.

The committee looked at each other with uncertainty but slowly they realised what was happening, *or what they hoped was happening.*

*

Emery wiped the blood from his face. "I think he broke my nose!" he moaned.

"Ahm nay gonna say ah told you so, but we could have saved a lot of time if we had just done it my way ti start with!" Jack stood back from the guards, their heaped and unconscious bodies on the floor to the left of the door. "Anyway, stop your whining, ah was the one who got the big bastard!"

"Well, mine wasn't exactly small!"

"Aye. It was a nice right hook you gave him to the neck by the way," Jack smiled.

"Okay, laugh it up. He was tall, I couldn't reach his face! He went down though, didn't he?" Emery had a rising feeling of pride, but it didn't stop his nose from hurting.

"Aye, he went doon like a sack of dropped shite! Credit where it's due, pal," Jack surveyed the damage to his knuckles on his right hand. It was minimal. "We'd better get a move on!"

No sooner had the words left his lips than the walls began to shake, slightly at first and then with more ferocity, causing stonework to loosen from the ceiling.

"What's that?" shouted Emery over the noise of the quake.

"Let's go!" answered Jack.

They pushed the door open and ducked through the doorway to avoid the falling masonry. The room that lay beyond was completely white. It was difficult to see through the brightness whether the walls were even made of stone, such was the
contrast from the stone corridors they had come from.

161

On the far side of the room there shimmered a slim red line in the wall. It crackled and spat sparks into the air.

"That's it!" shouted Emery.

They both scampered up to it as huge chunks of stone fell, smashing into acrid dust around them.

The shaking became more violent and was now accompanied by a high-pitched wailing noise.

They grabbed their ears quickly.

"Argh!" screamed Jack.

"What is it?" reeled Emery.

"God knows! Let's get oot of here!"

Hands still clamped firmly to their heads, they both dived into the portal, disappearing with a large snap of electricity. A second later, the portal imploded in a fiery burst of red, the stonework from the wall ricocheting around the floor in small, angry particles.

*

Bodin stood on as Enkil fell to his knees.

Enkil's eyes burned bright red, the veins in his neck were almost at bursting point as he screamed out the high-pitched frequency.

And at that point Bodin was proud to know the man. They would both surely be promoted for this!

162

The great hall was alive with falling stone and screaming. The soldiers had long since discarded their weapons to clutch at their ears, they themselves now were screaming at the intensity of the noise.

The committee had taken to crouching beneath the table to avoid being hit by the debris; they too were clutching their ears. They knew what was to come and even though it wouldn't affect them, the noise was still excruciating.

Sure enough, as they had expected, the soldiers began to fall one by one.

Blood began to seep from their eyes at first, the build-up of pressure within them forcing its way out and then from their noses and mouths. Trembling wildly, they soon began to implode. Their entire bodies being vacuumed in on themselves, being turned inside out with explosions of blood.

All around the hall screams of panic and agony clung to the stench of blood in the air, showers of splintered bone being thrown against pillars of claret stone.

Amid the sheer horror of it all Slarin remained standing, hands on ears. His black eyes began to fill with blood.

"Noooooooooooooooo!" he screamed.

The committee members looked on from beneath the table, all waiting for it to end.

And then, amongst the maelstrom of activity Slarin stood perfectly still and looked up at them.

"How you say, 'bollocks.'"

And then instantly he imploded, his eyeballs being heaved and thrown from his crushed carcass via two jets of blood, landing at the foot of the table like two steaming hard-boiled eggs, covered in chopped tomatoes.

What was left of his inside out corpse slumped to the floor in a slurry of flatulent organs and pissing veins and instantly the wailing stopped.

The hall stopped shaking and all fell silent.

Through the dust and blood, the committee members rose one by one from under the table and began to survey the aftermath around them.

Not too far from them, in a small, cold room, just off one of the many corridors that riddled the compound, Enkil finally took a deep breath as he lay, exhausted on the cold stone floor.

As he opened his eyes, he could see his breath rising through the cold air around him. He hadn't seen that in a long time, it felt good to be cold. Maybe he would get to keep this room.

He slowly sat up and looked at Bodin, who was knelt opposite, smiling.

"We did it buddy!" laughed Enkil, through the soreness of his throat. He coughed slightly at the discomfort. "Seriously," he looked at Bodin and pointed to the chalice. "Don't ever drink that stuff, it's grim!"

Through the elation and relief though, Enkil's thoughts were of Emery and Jack. He hoped they had made it through the portal.

A hunch told him they had.

Epilogue

The first thing Emery noticed was all the police tape where his windows had once been. Then he noticed all of the shattered glass and rubble.

"Shit."

The kitchen, the hall, the living room. All in need of a good deal more than a spot of spring-cleaning.

He walked down the hallway and peered into his bedroom to see his bed caked in glass and rubble, more police tape and yet again there was the absence of a window.

"Shit."

Emery hadn't expected to find the place tidy but was shocked at the level of devastation he had come home to.

He desperately tried running through excuses in his head to offer his landlord but the ideas section of his brain must have been sleeping.

Jack had been nosing around the place too and was also stunned at just how much damage the flat had sustained.

"Must have been quite a scrap, eh?"

Emery shook his head with disbelief.

"How can I explain this? The landlord's going to want some sort of explanation! *And* the police!"

Jack had checked the bathroom, whilst still keeping one ear open to listen to Emery's worries.

"Ah, thank Christ for that! At least the crapper's fine." He closed the door and patted Emery on the shoulder. "Listen, do nay try and take it all onboard now. Ah noticed a couple of beers still on the coffee table. Let's crack 'em open and just sit and be for a while."

"You're probably right," said Emery, wallowing in worry.

They wandered through the hall and into the living room and slumped into the settee.

"We've just been through a lot by the way, it takes a while ti get over that kind of thing."

Emery opened the two bottles of beer and passed one to Jack.

"Here's to getting out of Hell alive anyway," said Emery, clinking Jack's bottle with his own.

"Aye, here's ti that." They both had hearty mouthfuls of beer and put their feet up on the charred table in front of them.

Emery reached for the television remote. "Spot of telly?" he asked, switching it on.

166

"Why not?"

It was a surreal moment. After the experience they had just had, it seemed the most normal thing to do was to watch television. Under the circumstances Emery was quietly pleased and surprised that it still worked.

The set hummed into life and the two were presented with the news.

Emery almost choked on his beer.

There were live pictures of Wormsley and Sons Accountants being 'put out' by fire fighters.

"Shit."

THE END

No animals were harmed during the writing of this book.
At least not by the author.

Read the sequel to **Trouser's Edge** next…

ONCE UPON A HELL

Prologue

The night had drawn in quickly around the university. Surrounded as it was by dense woodland, it seemed to grow darker there before anywhere else in the town.

Professor Mayworth was still in his office, as usual.

He rarely left it these days, to the detriment of his teaching and his social life, such that it was. He had never enjoyed socialising even when his wife was alive. She had, of course insisted on it, at the very least once or twice a month and because he had loved her, he had conceded to her will.

Since her passing though, he had thrown himself ever more heavily into his work, seeking the solace of numbers and figures, so easily ordered and controlled.

Mathematics and physics were more than a job to him; they were a passion that had consumed his sixty years. He had always enjoyed solving puzzles and 'making things correct', even as a child. His choice to teach was in some part to spread the joy he felt for his vocation, but mainly it was a career that had allowed him to indulge his own obsession.

And it *was* an obsession.

Especially now.

Two months ago, he had hit upon a strange half equation in an old pagan text. It had been crudely scrawled into the corner of the binding and an ancient history professor had thought to ask him what it was.

It hadn't contained numbers or even mathematical symbols, certainly not as we would recognise them, but an equation it surely was. And he was almost on the brink of solving it, *at least he was sure that he was.*

As he stared at the blackboard in front of him, his eyes busily darting across the chalk numbers and symbols, he heard the creak of the cupboard door opening behind him.

He turned quickly to the corner of the room, but saw nothing but the darkness there staring back at him. Upon straining his eyes, he eventually made out a figure dressed in black, partly hidden in the shadows. It startled him, but he didn't look away, choosing instead to stare harder and longer to make out the details of what lurked there, and then he made out the eyes, though that was all he could see, those cold eyes boring into him from out of the darkness surrounding them.

The professor's mouth dried instantly. "Hello?"

The intruder remained statuesque and silent.

"What are you doing there, what do you want?"

"You." It answered in a deep, crackling voice.

"What, why?" The professor began to panic.

The stranger moved from out of the shadows, but somehow the darkness followed him, as if clinging to the man's clothes.

"Your genius it seems is your undoing. Curiosity killed the cat, Professor." The voice was sneering now and laced with an acid coldness.

"Who are you?" demanded the professor as the stranger reached beneath his dark cloak, removing a small, slender, silver pipe.

"I am Curiosity. Unfortunately for you, you are the cat."

With that the stranger put the pipe to his lips and blew. From the end of it shot a small, silver dart, which rapidly ended up in the professor's neck.

Within an instant, the professor was lying on the floor and a mere handful of seconds later he was dead.

THE SEQUEL TO TROUSER'S EDGE

ONCE
UPON
A HELL

AVAILABLE FROM DURGE PULP

CARL LEE

Carl Lee was born in Kings Lynn, England in 1975 and has since lived in numerous places from Germany to Yorkshire and Spain to Cyprus. He currently resides in Blackpool, England where he writes, mainly because it is too windy to go outside.

Printed in Great Britain
by Amazon